COLLIE JOLLY

LEIGH LANDRY

COLLIE JOLLY by Leigh Landry

Published by Leigh Landry

Lafayette, LA, USA

© 2019 Leigh Landry

This is a work of fiction. Names, characters, places, and incidents either are the products of the author's imagination or are used fictitiously.

Cover design by germancreative

CHAPTER 1

ASHLEY STARED AT THE PILE OF BUSINESS CASUAL CLOTHING occupying half of her bedroom floor. Slacks. Polyester blouses. A couple of fitted suit jackets. How fast would they go up in flames? How badly did she want back the damage deposit on her apartment?

Music. That's what she needed. A theme song.

She grabbed her phone and sent The Clash to her wireless speaker on the nightstand. It only took a few lines of blasting lyrics before her roommate appeared in the doorway.

Even though it was only seven-thirty, Theresa had already changed into her sweatpants, fuzzy reindeer socks, and a Tulane hoodie. Her hair was wrapped in a bright, rainbow paisley silk scarf, the bold colors playing gorgeously against her luminous, freshly moisturized light brown skin. Theresa waited tables at a busy touristy place near the Quarter, and she'd worked lunch shift today after two days of doubles before that. How she hadn't already crashed in bed, Ashley had no idea.

"What the heck is going on in here?"

"I'm getting rid of my work clothes. Not like I need them anymore." Ashley surveyed the pile. "Got any matches?"

Theresa scrunched her face and looked back and forth between the pile and Ashley.

"Kidding," Ashley said. But The Clash sang: *Robbin' people with a six-gun; I fought the law and the law won.* "Mostly?"

Theresa crossed her arms and cleared her throat as she leaned against the doorframe. "So instead of finding another job, you're going to...what? Burn your clothes and commit armed robbery?"

"Probably not." Well, at least not the felony part.

"What are you doing here anyway? It's the weekend after Thanksgiving."

Ashley temporarily put her life of crime on hold to flash her roommate a confused look. "What does that have to do with anything?"

"You don't spend a normal weekend evening in this bedroom, let alone the official start of the holidays: Peak Ashley Season. In all the years I've known you, I haven't once seen you in a bad mood in December, much less home on a Saturday night."

"Well, for one, it isn't December yet." She sighed. "And two, that's because my life hasn't been over in December before."

Theresa rolled her eyes. "Dramatic much?"

"I'm just getting started." Ashley plopped onto the edge of her bed.

Dramatic.

Dramatic would be curling up in a corner for weeks while pretending she hadn't been laid off without notice. When the oil industry went into yet another shitty plummet, the web development company she worked for lost a ton of work from those clients. Because apparently, no one gives a shit about sprucing up their websites when they're laying off people left and right across the state.

"Isn't there some post-Thanksgiving bash you can go to?"

Normally, Theresa would be on the right track. Nothing could drag Ashley out of a funk like surrounding herself with music and people. Especially new people. She could easily make a few calls, put on something sparkly, and head out for some mood-boosting fun.

But she didn't exactly have mood-boosting *funds* anymore. In fact, she didn't have funds at all now, unless she counted her savings. Which she was trying her best not to count on.

She'd had a plan before the layoff. Multiple plans. Five-year plans. Ten-year plans. Long-term retirement plans. None of those plans involved touching her as-yet meager savings. Certainly not for pick-me-up partying.

Heck, she had rented this tiny Bywater apartment, complete with a gorgeous view of…the *levee*, because the plan didn't include fancy Downtown digs. Not yet, at least. So she wasn't about to blow up her savings on partying while unemployed.

Unemployed.

Her boss had assured her they'd give her a call as soon as they got clients back if she didn't find work elsewhere in the meantime. Great, except no one knew how long this current industry recession would last. Could be months. Could be years.

"You know what you need?" Theresa sat on the bed beside Ashley and nudged her arm. "A cat."

Ashley let out a small laugh. Theresa had been campaigning for an apartment kitten for the last six months. Ashley was worried about the time and attention a kitten would require with both of them working so much, so

Theresa had shifted her pitch to an older cat. Something chill and mostly self-sufficient but still snuggly. Now that she was out of work, she lost ground on the we-don't-have-time-for-a-cat argument.

"You can't adopt a cat every time I listen to The Clash."

"No, but if you're listening to The Clash at the beginning of the holiday season, this feels like a cat emergency."

"There is no such thing as a cat emergency." Ashley tried to sound convincing. The whole cat thing was actually starting to sound like a solid plan.

Theresa lifted her legs slightly to wave her fuzzy reindeer socks in the air. "Want me to put on pants and go out with you?"

Ashley shook her head. It was the sweetest offer she'd probably ever heard—especially coming from the Queen of Homebodies who was clearly exhausted from a long week. "I appreciate it, but no."

"Listen." Theresa sighed. "I know you're bummed about work. But you'll find another job in no time."

Ashley snorted. "Yeah, right."

The health of oil and gas had an unfortunate ripple effect on every other industry in the area. Jobs, even tech jobs, would be hard to come by for a while. Particularly for someone young without connections. So much of how things got done in this city still boiled down to who you knew and who owed who favors.

Theresa nudged her arm. "Hey, come work with me. You know we're always turning over servers."

"That's not exactly a glowing endorsement."

"I can totally talk them into giving you some shifts until you find something more permanent."

Ashley leaned her head on her friend's shoulder. "Thanks. I'll keep that in mind."

Theresa kissed the top of her head. "Any time. Now, can we cut out the arson and punk anthems for the night? Maybe donate the clothes instead of getting us evicted?"

Ashley reached for her phone, which had switched over to the Ramones, to lower the volume. "Sorry. I'll keep my shenanigans down."

"I'm just worried about you." Theresa stood. "You need anything? Dance party? Ice cream and a rom-com?" She struggled to stifle a yawn and failed. "Puppy internet videos?"

Ashley had really lucked out three years ago when she'd come home early one day and found her shit-stain of an ex-boyfriend showering with her equally shitty ex-roommate. She'd promptly sent both their asses packing, and the universe sent her this sweet angel to pay half the rent. Theresa had quickly evolved into Ashley's best friend, confidant, and fleece-clad partner in crime.

"Thanks, but you should get some rest. I'll be fine."

Theresa looked exhausted but unconvinced. "Promise?"

"Promise."

"Okay, if you're sure. I'm going to snuggle up with a duke. I only have two chapters left with this one." She gave a weak wave before turning down the hall. "Goodnight."

"Goodnight."

With Theresa gone, Ashley looked back at her pile of clothes on the floor and stood to get a garbage bag from the kitchen. Packing them for a charity drop-off was probably a better plan than burning them. At least this way someone else could benefit from her failure.

By the time she returned with the bag and started stuffing the clothes inside, she'd decided maybe storing them in the closet for a while was an even better idea. Or at least a more frugal idea. Less satisfying than setting the pile on fire, but definitely more sensible. No point buying all new clothes if she would eventually get another job. Even if that was a year from now. Or more.

The thing that annoyed her most—aside from the obvious loss of the job itself—was that Theresa was right. This *was* Ashley Season.

It was the weekend after Thanksgiving. She should have been taking out a box of decorations instead of packing bags of clothes. She should have been hanging lights and garlands and putting out bowls of scented pinecones, but she wasn't at all in the mood for that right now. This was her favorite time of the year. And it was ruined.

Ashley abandoned the packing task and brought her laptop onto the bed. Surely she could find some other job in this city besides waiting tables. She'd done enough of that in college, and she wasn't exactly what anyone would call "good" at it.

She'd hoped she'd never have to do that again. Especially not in the French Quarter, where there was an endless parade of grabby tourists thinking the whole city was rule-free and consequence-free and that everyone living here existed purely for their pleasure. And since Ashley was the worst actress in the world, her true emotions always plainly painted on her face, she could never hide her disgust or rage. That didn't exactly translate to tips.

She pulled up a job site and scrolled through for anything in web development or design that she might be even remotely qualified for. Everything she found—including the entry-level positions—required five-plus years of experience. She had three. Four if she stretched and fudged. She'd apply for those anyway, but with everyone losing jobs lately, the current level of job market competition wouldn't leave that kind of resume wiggle room.

She sighed and stared at the empty stretch of the bed

beside her. Maybe a cat wasn't such a bad idea. She could sure use some pets and purrs right about now. And her jobless butt wouldn't exactly entice a whole lot of human snuggle potential. Sure, she could probably find a warm body on a dating app, but random lonely hookups weren't on the five-year plan.

Neither was a cat, though.

Ashley went back to scrolling and expanded her search to everything available in the area. In between the tech listings, she found plenty of openings in hospitality (see: worst actress evidence above) and retail (see: same evidence). She also found a million ads for nurses and nursing techs. Even if her bedside manner wasn't worse than her tableside manner, she couldn't have her own blood drawn without getting lightheaded and nauseated. No way could she carry around trays of other people's blood or change nasty bed sheets.

She was ready to give up when a different listing caught her eye.

Dog walker.

Huh. Maybe? Definitely not on the five-year plan, but it could keep her from dipping into her retirement fund at the ripe age of twenty-five.

And…whoa. That pay couldn't be right.

She opened the listing and read the description. No formal requirements, not even a "must love dogs" clause. But the job was more than just dog walking. They wanted training too. Ashley had never trained a dog in her life. She'd never even had a dog as a kid.

But she liked dogs. And she'd always wanted one. Her home life had been a mess when she was a kid, and the thing that stuck out to her about all her friends whose parents stayed together and didn't fight or shuffle their kids from house to house was that they all had a family dog. A dog was most definitely on the ten-year plan.

She decided she could handle walking a dog, and it couldn't be *that* hard to teach a dog to sit. Right? There were books for that. With instructions. She could read and follow instructions and hang out with a cute dog.

She typed an email, perky but professional, pitching herself as a seasoned dog person. Then she attached her resume and hoped they wouldn't look at it. She couldn't possibly manipulate its contents to make it appear that she was even remotely qualified for this job.

Still, she had a good feeling. Maybe it was almost-December vibes. Christmas magic was totally a thing. And if anyone deserved a little of that magic right now, Ashley did.

With a lighter heart, Ashley closed the laptop and returned to packing her clothes. As she put the last pair of slacks in the bag and stuffed it in the closet, her phone rang. It was an unknown local number.

"Hello?"

"Hi, is this Ashley?" The voice was feminine with a sharp edge.

"Yes."

"Hi Ashley, I'm Madison. I'm calling about the dog walking position you inquired about."

That was fast. She didn't expect to hear anything for at least a week. "Did I forget to include something?" Weird that they wouldn't just email to ask her for more information or references or whatever.

"No, no, no," the woman said. "This all looks good. I was calling to see if we could set up an interview."

Ashley was surprised the woman had had time to read her email, much less look over her resume. "An interview? Absolutely. When would be a good time for you?"

"How about tomorrow morning?"

"Sure," Ashley stammered. "That would be fine. Great, I mean! Um, what time and where would you like to meet?"

"How about Crescent Cafe? The big coffee shop on Magazine? It's a few blocks from my place and has outdoor seating, so I can meet you there with Bacchus. The dog. How about there at nine?"

The woman's words fell out quickly and had an air of insistence and hope hanging from them. Her voice was that just-right pitch—slightly low for a woman's voice—that Ashley just adored.

She pulled the phone away from her ear and shook her head. Jeez. She wasn't looking for a date here. Especially not with someone who could potentially be her boss. *That* wasn't in any plan.

"Sounds great. I'm looking forward to meeting you and Bacchus."

"Great! Me too. I'll see you at nine tomorrow morning. I'll be the one with the Border Collie."

A Border Collie. At least she knew what those looked like. Not much else about them, other than they were adorable.

"Looking forward to it!" she said. "See you then."

Ashley shook off her daydreams of wandering the city with an adorable dog and getting paid for it.

First, she had to ace an interview.

This was turning out better than she could have hoped. She could potentially get paid to basically exercise and hang out with a dog. *And* she would be having coffee with the woman who owned that delicious voice.

Focus, Ashley.

Coffee with the dog. Yes, the dog and the job were what mattered here.

With her spirits lifted and hope in her heart, Ashley raced to the closet to dig for the perfect interview outfit.

CHAPTER 2

A BITING GUST OF COLD AIR CUT ACROSS MADISON'S FACE AS she turned the corner at the end of the block onto Magazine Street. She was practically running toward the coffee shop, but not because of the cold and certainly not by choice.

Bacchus jogged a couple feet ahead of her, the leash taut, dragging her the whole way. The puppy—technically he was a year old, but still very much a puppy most days—glanced back at her every few feet with pure joy on his face. His jubilance might have been infectious...*if* the flea magnet hadn't been yanking her arm out of its socket.

When they reached the coffee shop, Madison started to panic for a second. All the outdoor tables were taken, even with the massive cold front that had just swooped through the area. She normally came here during the week, and she forgot to take into account how busy it might be on a Sunday morning. Especially on a holiday weekend. Lots of locals and tourists alike were out and about shopping downtown, which was close enough to attract plenty of extra foot traffic.

It wasn't even December yet, and she was already a mess.

How was she going to get through the anniversary if she couldn't even make it through November with her mind intact?

A woman sitting alone stood and flashed a great big smile at them. "Madison?" she asked.

"Yes. Ashley?" Bacchus tangled the leash as he excitedly sniffed all around the woman's legs. She wore skinny black pants, a crisp blue button-down shirt, and shiny flats that didn't look comfortable enough for walking a dog.

"Yes." She pushed her big, dark sunglasses on top of her head, perching them on her sleek raven-black hair, and extended her hand. "Nice to meet you."

"You too." Madison shook her hand, then gestured down at the tangle of leash and dog caught in the cafe chair legs. She gritted her teeth and held back a gigantic sigh. "And *this* is Bacchus."

Ashley crouched beside the chair and let the dog sniff her hand. Then she pet him and tried to coax him out. When he only got himself more stuck, she reached for the leash. "May I?"

Madison handed over the end of the leash, thankful someone else could handle the untangling for once. Ashley wove the leash through the web and freed Bacchus a few seconds later. He showered her with sloppy, excited kisses in thanks. Madison said a silent apology to the woman's perfectly applied makeup, now smudged and shining with dog slobber.

"How about I let you two get acquainted while I grab drinks for us. What can I get you? They make the best pour-over, but everything is delicious here."

"That sounds great." Ashley barely looked up, completely smitten with the bundle of black and white floof, now perched halfway on her lap. Madison felt a smile tugging at the corner of her mouth, and her heart raced at the sight.

But the joy quickly evaporated as she realized why it made her so happy. Who this scene reminded her of. And what could have been.

Madison rushed inside and steadied herself against the door as she closed it behind her. The coffee shop was even busier inside, and the high brick walls bounced the conversations and brewing noises furiously throughout the open space while instrumental jazz versions of Christmas songs blasted from speakers. But the smell of coffee in the air was soothing, as was the serenity of a brief respite from that beast outside. Not to mention a break from those unwelcome memories.

While she waited in line to place their order, Madison peeked out the big front window where she could see her interviewee talking animatedly to Bacchus as he smiled and panted his doggy breath in her face. Between the decorative spray frost on the edges of the window framing the pair and the perfect morning lighting, Madison wished she'd brought her camera along with her.

A few minutes later, she returned to their spot outside with two disposable cups. The chill in the air had painted Ashley's cheeks and pointy, little nose with a subtle rosy blush.

Madison tried not to stare at her crystal blue eyes. She was like a high contrast portrait, the kind of complexion that sparkled in jewel tones. Such a stark contrast to her memories of Callie, who always fully embraced her paleness, complimenting her wavy red hair and cool freckled skin with muted pastel dresses.

Ashley's hair fell over her shoulders while she scratched the dog's face and laughed. There was a lightness to this woman's personality and an ease with Bacchus that no matter how much she wanted to ignore it, Madison couldn't help but notice the similarity. That hint of childlike joy that brought back so many memories.

Or maybe it was just this time of year. The upcoming month would surely be even more unrelenting in its reminders. Among which, the reminder that laughter and lightness and magic and joy were for other people.

Madison looked down at where Bacchus now sat on the woman's shiny shoes, panting at people as they walked past. She handed Ashley her drink. "You two getting along, I see?"

"Thank you." Ashley took a whiff of the steam and set the hot drink on the table. "We're definitely buddies now."

"Good." Madison tapped her short, neatly trimmed fingernails on her mug. "I'm uh, not great with small talk, so should we jump right into things?"

Ashley flinched ever so slightly but maintained her cool, professional vibe. She flashed a confident smile and said, "Sure."

"Well, I believe the question of whether or not Bacchus likes you has been answered." Bacchus reiterated his approval by licking Ashley's hand. Repeatedly. Madison tugged at his leash until he stopped. But only momentarily.

"He's fine," Ashley said. "I don't mind a little dog slobber with my coffee."

"That's good because he's got plenty to share." Madison cleared her throat and dove into the one thing that had been bothering her ever since she opened that email and file. "I saw from your resume you've done a lot of tech work before now. What drew you to apply for this job?"

"Well, I've always loved dogs."

Ashley paused her speech to take a tiny sip of coffee. While she was clearly stalling for some reason, she maintained her composure and didn't give even a whiff of a hint that she might be flustered by the question.

She placed her cup back on the table and reestablished eye contact with Madison. "To be completely honest, my company had several big oil and gas accounts and recently laid off a lot of employees. The job market pushed me to branch out a bit." She flashed a thousand-watt smile and nodded toward Bacchus. "After meeting this guy, I'm honestly glad for that push."

Madison was mesmerized by that smile. That wide, bright smile and those shiny, peach-tinted lips. Madison was so enchanted she nearly lost her entire train of thought. And the fact that this was an interview.

"So the job history is accurate?" she said. "You don't have any past experience with dog training? Or any animal-related field, for that matter?"

For the first time, Ashley's confident demeanor faltered. She blinked rapidly a couple of times while she wet her lips and shifted in her seat. Her wind-chilled cheeks paled a bit, but she was still stunning.

Madison looked down at her coffee cup and rubbed her thumb along the handle, reminding herself that she wasn't here to gawk at an attractive woman. She was here to hire a dog walker and trainer, and she wasn't sure if this woman could even do the job.

Not to mention she didn't date employees. Or even potential employees.

"The resume is accurate," Ashley finally said, with a firm but humble tone. "I don't have any formal training or experience. But I'm eager, I love dogs, I'm a quick learner, and I am tenacious when put to any test."

Madison didn't personally know a thing about this woman, but she believed every word coming out of her mouth. She truly believed that this person could wake up one morning, decide to be a dog trainer, and make that happen.

More importantly, she was here. Bacchus liked her. And Madison didn't have time to wait around for someone else to apply. She'd been trying to find a new owner for Bacchus for weeks, but he was such a mess that she'd finally realized she needed to put him through some kind of puppy boot camp first. And she was not the one to do that. So, if she was going to get rid of him before the end of the year and get a fresh start, she needed someone to work with him. *Anyone.*

A truck pulling a fishing boat drove by, and Bacchus did his thing. He darted toward the road, yanking Madison's arm with him, and began a tirade of hysterical barking and lunging.

The sooner the better.

When the truck and boat were out of earshot and Bacchus settled back onto the ground, Madison exhaled and looked across the table at Ashley. To her credit, Ashley seemed mostly unfazed. Madison wished she could say the same of herself.

"How would you like to walk him back to my apartment?"

ASHLEY TRIED to follow Madison down Magazine Street, but her new ward had other ideas. She really hoped this dog knew how to get home because no matter how hard she tried, she could not convince him to slow down. They barreled through shoppers and couples taking long, leisurely weekend strolls through the neighborhood, while Ashley cheerfully apologized over her shoulder for jostling them and practically knocking half of them over.

So far, she was really acing this interview.

It didn't look like she'd be doing much holiday shopping. Not after this craptastic performance. In less than five minutes, she was proving herself the worst dog walker ever. And they hadn't even moved on to the training part of the job yet. Ashley was doomed.

The good thing about being ahead of Madison was that Ashley couldn't be tempted to stare creepily at the tall, beautiful woman who happened to be her potential boss. Or maybe not, after this little stroll.

Ashley's arm flailed as Bacchus darted from side to side, sniffing every storm drain, trashcan, and butt along the way. There was a *lot* to smell. Not as much in this neighborhood as other parts of the city, but the Lower Garden District still had its fair share of interesting "stuff" to explore. Especially for an exuberant young dog.

They turned a corner and Madison pointed ahead. "It's right up here on the left."

Ashley followed Madison's finger and spotted the small, pale yellow duplex. It was cute and tidy but unassuming. Kind of like Madison.

She followed Madison and Bacchus inside, although she wasn't sure why. There was no way she would get this job. Not after this bouncing clown of a dog dragged her for three blocks and tangled himself in both their legs *and* nearly took out an old lady with the leash slack.

It was official. Ashley was the worst dog walker on the face of the planet.

Madison's house was dark inside—dark carpet, dark wood shelves, dark furniture—and the shut-tight curtains didn't help the matter. Madison flicked on a couple lamps, which gave a warm, sophisticated glow to the room, but didn't exactly brighten the place.

The lamps did illuminate the huge photographs covering

the walls. Gorgeous, vibrant snapshots of the city and the people who live and work in it. Like a tribute wall to the lesser-known parts of New Orleans. The *real* New Orleans.

"Are these yours?" she asked, stepping close to one with Bacchus's leash still loose in hand as he drank noisily from a nearby water dish.

"Yes," Madison answered. "Can I get you a water or anything?"

"No, thank you. They're gorgeous. Are you a professional photographer?"

Ashley didn't know any photographers. She didn't know many creative types at all, really. Besides Theresa, all of her friends were fellow web and tech geeks or small business owners, people who talked about the changing face of social media and brand building and the latest finance management software. They didn't talk much about art. Ashley's education had included a single required music appreciation class, but she could still spot beauty, and she could tell when something radiated skill and talent. This woman clearly had both.

"Yes, but mostly weddings and senior portraits. Things like that. These are just for fun, I guess."

"They really are beautiful," Ashley repeated.

"Thank you." She blushed a little, then reached to grab the leash. She unhooked Bacchus and hung the leash on a hook near the front door. Beneath the now dangling leash sat a pair of running shoes…or what looked like might have once been running shoes. The soles and half of one heel seemed to have been mauled by a wild animal.

A heavy mass of fur plopped onto Ashley's feet. Bacchus panted and smiled up at her, clearly proud of himself, his handiwork, and his choice of seat.

Now she understood the training part of the job description.

Too bad Ashley didn't know a single thing about how to keep a dog from chewing shoes. This was so far beyond sit-stay, and Bacchus wasn't exactly the tiny puppy she'd imagined from the job description. Which meant he was probably a whole lot more stubborn. They weren't in old-dog-new-tricks territory, but she was still way out of her league here. Not that she had a league to begin with.

"Well," Madison said, "now that you and Bacchus are acquainted, I guess we can talk details." She gestured at the living room. "Shall we sit and discuss?"

Ashley hesitated but followed and sat in a bright blue, low profile armchair with Bacchus plopping down to rest against her leg. At least he was rooting for her.

"As you've seen, Bacchus is…spirited?"

Ashley grinned. That was one way to put it. "He does have a lot of energy." Way too much energy to be locked up in this apartment all day. She could easily see why someone busy would need help with him. But if Madison was a photographer and worked from home, wouldn't she have a flexible schedule? At least flexible for dog walks? "But he's very sweet." She winked at Bacchus, who panted and smiled wider, like he knew she had his back too.

"Sweet." Madison looked dubiously at Bacchus. "Sure."

Ashley couldn't blame her for the hint of resentment in Madison's voice and in the look she gave him. The dog had eaten her shoes.

Or someone else's shoes?

Ashley immediately scanned the room for signs that someone else lived here. Not that it mattered. But she needed to know if she'd also be answering to anyone else.

Or at least that was the story she was telling herself.

All her quick visual search revealed were bookshelves and photographs of what looked like strangers. No framed personal shots on those bookshelves or anywhere else. No extra coats by the door.

"I've neglected his training for way too long, so his behavior is partially on me. Despite the circumstances."

Ashley couldn't miss the sudden tightness in Madison's voice or the word "circumstances." But she decided it wasn't her place to pry. Certainly not now, when they'd just met. "Well, I think you have a fabulous dog here. Handsome *and* bright. Even if he's a little enthusiastic."

"He isn't mine."

Ashley froze. Had she been wrong about someone else not living there?

"Sorry." Madison shut her eyes tightly, took a breath, then slowly opened them again. "I guess he is. For now." She paused another moment, opening and closing her mouth a couple times as if debating what to say. "He was my girlfriend's. She got him last year."

"Oh." Girlfriend. Well, that explained that. Ashley tried to ignore the tiny ember of disappointment scorching her stomach. She had nothing to be disappointed about. Well, nothing except the fact that she'd completely botched her dog walking test. But her potential boss's girlfriend was absolutely none of her business, and certainly nothing to be disappointed about.

Madison frowned and stared at the dog. "She died last year, about a month after she got him."

Damn.

And that explained that. The lack of decorations. The lack of personal photos. The lack of puppy training. The lack of...*everything*.

"I'm so sorry." Ashley couldn't bear to look at Madison, so she looked down at Bacchus, who also seemed to pick up on the tension and had draped himself sadly over Ashley's feet.

Madison cleared her throat. "So, here we are. I've got a year-old dog with all the energy of a puppy who needs more space than the inside of this apartment can provide and more attention and discipline than I can provide." She forced a smile, and Ashley saw all the hope Madison was clutching in that one expression. All of the hope she was stuffing into this one interview. "That's where you come in."

"Are you sure?" Ashley shook her head. What was she doing? She'd never talked herself out of a job before, and she sure as heck didn't need to start now. Not when she was jobless and way off track on her long-term goals. "I mean, I didn't think I exactly aced the whole walking thing."

"Are you kidding?" Madison laughed. "You should see when *I* walk him. I've taken out more than my fair share of little old ladies on these sidewalks, I promise."

They both laughed, and Madison's face lightened for just a moment. It was a lovely sight. Ashley guessed there hadn't been a whole lot of laughter for her over the last year.

"But he'll need multiple walks every day, or at least two long walks. You can set your schedule for those. And I'll want you to work with him here. Help me train him. Give him some structure and tricks to keep his mind occupied. Dog's too smart for his own good."

Ashley at least knew that about the breed after reading up on it last night. Border Collies needed jobs and tasks and tricks to keep them feeling useful and mentally stimulated, in addition to burning off that physical energy. She didn't know the first thing about the chewing, but she considered herself pretty smart. At least half as smart as this dog. Surely she could find training videos and books to deal with that.

"When would you need me to start?"

Madison smiled again, and relief settled onto her face as

her muscles visibly relaxed. "Today? The job's yours if you want it."

Ashley looked down at Bacchus again, who was looking up expectantly for her answer. She swore that dog could understand their entire conversation.

She stood, as did Madison, and extended her arm for a handshake. "You and Bacchus have got yourselves a trainer."

CHAPTER 3

A WEEK LATER, STANDING IN THE MIDDLE OF ANNUNCIATION Square just after noon, Ashley finally came to the conclusion that she was the worst dog trainer in the history of dog trainers.

After a week of exhausting neighborhood walks and training on basic commands in Madison's living room, Ashley had figured it was time to step things up. So that Saturday, the first of December, she met Bacchus for a midday walk to the little park a few blocks from Madison's house.

She didn't even want to teach him anything new, just practice the basic commands the little smartypants had picked up quickly that week. Bacchus had been a quick learner and an eager pupil so far. No surprise. Border Collies were notoriously bright, but they could also be willful, mischievous, and stubborn. So today, she only wanted to add in one tiny new element to his training and practice the stuff he already knew in a public setting to see if he could maintain his focus.

Short answer: no, he most definitely could not.

Assumption Center Park had a super chill vibe for a Saturday. Not that she knew what this little green space nestled between two neighborhoods was normally like, since this wasn't an area of the city she typically hung out in. Too residential. Too…family oriented. The park had a few kids playing soccer—so much doggy temptation there—in the grassy field. A couple with a dog—Bacchus's new archfoe, apparently—sitting on a bench beneath the oak trees. Exactly the kinds of low-level distractions she had been looking for, but unfortunately even low-level was too much for Bacchus. Or too much for her.

She was inevitably the one who was failing here. Bacchus was just being…Bacchus. She was the one who was supposed to help him. She was the one who was supposed to do her job. She was the one who was supposed to *fix* Bacchus and Madison.

She had no idea how the heck she would do that last one, but over the last week, she felt more and more compelled every day to help these two figure things out.

Her phone buzzed in her back pocket. After making sure she had a firm grip on the leash with one hand while Bacchus took a break in the grass, she pulled out her phone and looked at the text from Theresa.

T: How's it going?

Ashley considered for a moment whether her friend wanted the real answer to that question. Theresa wasn't one to politely say anything simply for the sake of small talk, and she certainly wasn't the kind of person to ask a question only for the sake of opening a door to tell her own story. No, if Theresa asked a question, she legitimately wanted the answer. The *real* answer.

A: I hate this dog. (jk sort of)

T: Liar

A: This might be the only dog in the world I truly hate.

T: You haven't met enough dogs to have a dependable sample size for that kind of conclusion & I still need pics

That had been the first thing Theresa asked after Ashley's interview last week. Is the dog cute? Of course he was cute, but all Ashley had wanted to talk about was his even cuter owner.

She snapped a quick photo of Bacchus and his ever-present doggy smile and sent it to Theresa. A few seconds later, her predictable reaction arrived.

T: You are such a liar! It's scientifically impossible to hate that face

A: Spend ten minutes in a park with him and see how your tune changes.

T: Nonsense he looks like a very good boy. The bestest boy

A: The bestest boy who doesn't listen and is going to get me fired.

T: This is why we should get a cat, you wouldn't have to train a cat

Ashley laughed and shook her head at her phone. "Can you believe this?" she asked Bacchus. He plopped onto the grass and rolled on his side in answer.

A: That is quite possibly the worst reasoning for getting a cat I have ever heard. Even from you.

T: And yet, it's a fact. But seriously, if anyone can do this...you can. I've never seen you not do anything you set your mind to

A: Thanks. Really. <3

T: Now get back to training while I search rescue sites for our new roommate...

A: Theresa. No.

T: Can't talk now, cat searching, bye, good luck!!!

Booms echoed from downtown, and Ashley gripped

Bacchus's leash tightly as he jumped to his feet and barked, wildly searching for the source of the noise. A few seconds later, horns blared in the distance, muted by the buildings and traffic between them and the park. The Christmas parade. Krewe of Jingle. Thankfully, it wouldn't pass anywhere near them, but clearly, their training session was over.

After several minutes of tugging and pleading, Ashley managed to navigate Bacchus out of the park. She aimed them toward Madison's house and began their walk back, steeling herself to explain to her boss that she was a complete and utter failure.

MADISON STARED at the gorgeous new logo on her website header and tilted her head at the computer screen. Then she tilted her head to the other side. Yup. Definitely off-center. Still. No matter what she tried, she could not get the darn thing just right.

A thump at the front door grabbed her attention. Bacchus. Slamming his front paws on the door. She knew that sound all too well. Three soft knocks followed, and Madison opened the door for the pair a few moments later. The door was unlocked, but she knew by now that Ashley wouldn't walk in without knocking first.

Bacchus barreled through the door, dragging Ashley behind him. His behavior was much better lately, and his improvement in just a week with Ashley had been seriously impressive, but he still had a way to go before he would be fit for anyone else after a year of neglect. She only had herself to blame for that, but she was doing the right thing now. She was fixing what she'd broken, and every day she didn't have to walk that thing was a day she was grateful Ashley had entered their lives.

"How'd it go?" she asked.

Ashley bent to remove Bacchus's leash and hung it by the door. "Well, it went."

It pained Madison to hear that note of defeat in her voice. Their first public training session had obviously not gone the way Ashley had hoped. Madison wasn't at all surprised, but Ashley was always so optimistic and cheerful and determined. Disappointment, even a tiny bit, weighed so heavily on her.

Then, she realized the day and the warning she'd given Ashley just before they left. "Oh, gosh. You didn't run into the parade, did you?"

Madison shook her head. She still had her coat on. Not that Madison expected her to stay. She was there to work, not keep her company.

"No, we could hear it just before we came back, but it was far away," she said. "It just…didn't go as well as I'd planned."

Madison pressed her lips together to hold back a grin. From day one, Ashley had come in with a plan. She seemed to live a life of plans on top of plans and an endless string of goals and checkboxes and militant optimism. Despite Madison's warnings, Ashley had no idea she was facing her nemesis: Bacchus, the plan-killer.

She wanted to take some of the pressure off Ashley, to tell her that all she really needed was for him to behave enough so they could hand him off to someone else. He needed to be well behaved inside, he needed some structure and boundaries, and he needed to be able to walk without taking out half the neighborhood in the process. Madison didn't need him to be perfectly behaved in a park or in crowds. Someone else could worry about that later.

But Ashley and Bacchus had grown so attached to each other so quickly this week, Madison didn't think she'd handle the news well that this gig was temporary or that Bacchus was on limited time there. She knew she needed to be honest about that soon, but she couldn't pile that on top of the disappointment already clear on Ashley's face.

"It was the first try. Everything was new," Madison reassured her. "I'm sure the excitement will wear off a little next time."

Ashley shot her a look of doubt, then they both looked at Bacchus shaking his stuffed lamb toy.

"Okay," Madison added. "Maybe not. But I have faith in you."

"Well, at least one of us does." Ashley sighed and looked at her feet, then shook her head. When she re-established eye contact, her determined gaze was back. "I'm sorry. I don't mean to mope. I'll turn Bacchus into the perfect fluffy gentleman. I promise."

Her optimism was downright infectious. Madison almost believed every word of it. She would have if she hadn't already known Bacchus. "I'll settle for him not eating my shoes."

Ashley smiled. "Next on the list."

"Can I get you something before you leave? Something to warm you after that walk?" It was warm for early December, but the wind was still cold and cutting and Ashley had spent nearly two hours out in it. "Some tea? Hot chocolate?"

"No thanks," Ashley said. "I need to get back and change."

"Right. It's Saturday. I'm sure you must have plans." Madison easily forgot that other people have plans on the weekends. She couldn't remember the last time she had weekend plans other than binging some new series on TV.

"Nothing fancy. Just going to the Algiers bonfire with some friends."

"Oh, nice. I've never been to that. Always said we'd go see the bonfires along the river one year on Christmas Eve, but never did it."

Ashley bit her lip and paused for a second. "Do you have plans tonight? I have a friend who lives on the west bank so we park at his place and bring folding chairs to the levee and hang out. There's a band, but it's really low key. You're welcome to join us."

"That sounds nice."

Madison was surprised at how nice that really did sound. She hadn't even hung out with her own friends much lately. They used to have gatherings and dinner parties and attended cocktail hours and concerts together…but after last year, she didn't have the energy for much. She stopped hosting things, but she stopped joining her friends for things too. Soon, the invites stopped coming.

She'd never really liked hanging out with people she didn't know—she'd always been much more comfortable in small groups with close friends—but sitting by a bonfire with Ashley and her friends was shockingly tempting. The thought of it gave her a sudden, overwhelming desire to know what kinds of people Ashley hung out with. Who did she confide in? Who made her laugh and how? All the questions a boss most certainly did not ask about an employee.

Madison pulled her thoughts together and aimed a thumb at the computer desk in the corner of the living room. "Thanks for the invite, but I've got a hot date with my website."

Ashley looked at the computer. "Updating your business page?"

"Yeah, I need to update some plug-ins and back up the

site." She felt her body get heavier with every word. She hated this stuff. "I really need to update everything while I've got a light schedule this week. My design, my information, the whole thing. Ugh, it's taking me forever. I'm the worst at all of this."

"If you want, I could help with some of that." She put her hands up in defense. "Sorry, don't mean to overstep here. I mean, if you get stuck and need or want help, I'd be glad to."

"Oh, I couldn't—"

"You absolutely could," Ashley said. "Seriously. I'd be glad to."

Madison felt a buzz run through her at the sight of Ashley's warm, inviting smile. "Thanks. I appreciate that. I'll work on it some more today and let you know if I need a hand."

"Good," Ashley said. "Are you sure I can't convince you to take a break and watch stuff burn with us?"

Madison nodded. She needed the break, gosh did she, but this was a boundary she wasn't going to overstep. No matter how much she wanted to. "I'm sure. But thank you."

"Okay. If you change your mind, just text me. Always room for more on the levee!"

Madison smiled and walked Ashley out. She'd noticed herself smiling a lot more lately with Ashley around, and it wasn't just because Bacchus wasn't such a jerk anymore. That helped, but it was more because Ashley's mere presence in a room made the world feel lighter somehow.

As she waved goodbye from the porch while Ashley started up her practical gray sedan, Madison realized she couldn't remember the last time she felt this light or free or...*almost* happy. When the car drove off down the street, she shook her head and hugged her sweater tightly around her body, blocking out the chilly breeze that had kicked up and cut across her front porch.

But the breeze was the least of her problems right now. She went inside and closed the door, shutting out the cold December air. But there was no door to shut out her growing attraction to Ashley. She would have to figure out how to ward that off all on her own.

CHAPTER 4

ASHLEY PULLED THE LEGAL PAD, PEN, AND BOOK FROM HER tote bag and placed them in her lap. She covered them with her hands to hold them in place, then pushed herself gently on the big, metal porch-style swing overlooking the river. A heavy blanket of gray clouds covered the area as a chill prompted Ashley to wrap her jacket tighter. A perfectly dreary day to stare out across the water.

She didn't like waiting near Theresa's restaurant on the edge of the Quarter, even if she could find an empty bench outside. Too many tourists. Too much noise. Too much… everything. All of that was the New Orleans of TV commercials and web ads and brochures. Those tourists and that noise fed the city and its people. But there was so much more to New Orleans than all of that.

That's why she found herself out at Crescent Park time and time again. It sure as hell wasn't any safer to sit here, and it certainly wasn't what most people would call "pretty." It was a long, linear space carved out between the river and the decay of the city, the bottom edge of gentrification and neighborhoods filled with short-term rentals.

But peace lived here. As much as Ashley craved lights and music and decorations, especially during the holidays, she needed this place too. She needed the quiet, where all she could hear was the sound of runners' shoes on the pavement and the river sloshing against the Mandeville Wharf. Later in the day, soft Dixieland jazz danced in the air from the steamboat running its river tours. Sure, it smelled like mud and garbage and sometimes dog crap from rude short-term renters not picking up after their morning walks, but it was *real*. When she was working all the time in a brightly lit cubicle, she needed to get out here once in a while and bathe herself in the sights and smells and sounds of the tangible world.

Ashley returned her attention to the book in her lap. *Dog Training for Dummies*. She'd picked it up from the library a few days ago after she'd watched and bookmarked every dog training video she could find on the internet. She had some better books on hold and a couple on order, but this one had worked so far to help her create an initial training plan.

She'd given up on park training, for now, and refocused her attention this past week on discouraging him from chewing. She bought him new chew toys, hid Madison's remaining "good" shoes, and coated the chewed up ones with bitter spray. They spent some extra time just hanging out in the living area after mini-training sessions, so Ashley could catch him in the act and correct his behavior if he went for the shoes.

It worked, and within just a couple days, he wouldn't touch the shoes by the door. Yesterday Ashley even tested him by bringing out some of Madison's newer, in-tact footwear and swapping them for the bitter, chew-ed up ones. He barely even gave them a glance. In less than a week, she'd cured him of one of his most obnoxious habits. Or at least his most expensive one.

So now it was time to move on to a new trick. She wasn't at all looking forward to distraction training again, but eventually, they'd have to give that another shot. Maybe this weekend.

A tall woman approached from the side, and Ashley looked up to make sure it was the bright ray of sunshine she had been waiting for.

Theresa stood over her wearing a black polo shirt and her tight curls held off her forehead with a gold paisley scarf serving as a headband. She held up a brown paper bag and shook it gently in the air as she approached and plopped onto the bench beside Ashley. The smell of seafood and fry oil wafted under Ashley's nose as Theresa pulled out a gigantic, paper-wrapped sandwich. The little Creole restaurant Theresa worked at might be known for its gumbo, shrimp creole, and jambalaya, but this gem of a sandwich was the real star of the menu as far as Ashley was concerned. Especially since they took turns buying it on Theresa's discount.

Ashley grabbed a stack of napkins from the bag as Theresa unwrapped the fried shrimp and oyster po-boy and handed half to Ashley. Shredded lettuce poured out of the sides, but Ashley didn't waste a second to shove a corner into her mouth before any of that delicious seafood coupling tumbled out.

Theresa nodded at the book and legal pad in Ashley's lap. "Your new boss being a taskmaster?" She attacked her sandwich and ripped off a big bite.

"No. Madison's great. I swear, I even saw her smile at Bacchus the other day. It was the cutest thing too. She has this one little freckle that raises every time she smiles, and I swear her eyes literally sparkle."

Theresa froze mid-chew, staring at Ashley, then resumed and swallowed. "I was referring to your boss the dog." She tilted her head and gave a judgmental look. "But maybe we should discuss this gushing word avalanche about your person-boss instead."

Crap.

"What, I can't like my boss?"

"Like how?"

"Not like that."

Theresa smirked. "Sure."

"Seriously." Ashley dabbed a napkin at some mayo on the side of her mouth. "For one, she's my boss."

"Go on. Let's pretend I'm the one who needs convincing that crushing on this Madison person is a bad idea."

Ashley thought while she took another bite. And she thought some more. She thought about how Madison always wore tank tops inside her apartment, and how her long, iron-straight hair dangled over her bare shoulders. Then she thought about how Madison had this confident ease about her, more than just being comfortable in her apartment surrounded by her stuff. She was comfortable in her skin in a way Ashley couldn't really relate to. But how all of that confidence dissolved when she talked about doing anything outside of her house.

"Mm-hmm," Theresa said, wadding up the sandwich wrapper and tossing it into the empty bag.

Ashley let out a heavy sigh. "I don't have time for a relationship."

"Never stopped you before." Theresa eyed her warily.

"And look where that got me." Her last relationship hadn't been to blame for her layoff, but she couldn't help wondering if she hadn't been so busy trying to make things work with her ex all summer that maybe she would have been more productive at work. Sure, she'd put in tons of hours, more than anyone else in her department, but maybe she'd been distracted. Maybe she could have done more. Maybe she could have made herself more indispensable, so when the layoffs came late that fall they would have found a way to keep her on staff.

"So you plan on never dating anyone again? Ever?"

"At least not until I get back on track," she said. This whole dog training thing couldn't last forever, and she really needed to start sending out resumes again. Hopefully, the industry would pick up again early next year and there'd be some openings eventually. She needed to stay focused.

"Not even a holiday fling?"

Ashley laughed. A holiday fling sounded as delicious as hot chocolate and Christmas karaoke, but she needed this job. She wasn't about to lose it just because her boss was cute. "Especially not a holiday fling."

Theresa frowned, but she clearly recognized a losing argument when she saw one. "Well then, that leaves room in your life for only one thing."

"What?"

Theresa gave a wide, mischievous grin. "A cat." She pulled out her phone and showed the screen.

Ashley reeled back at the sight of the cream-colored blur climbing a cage door, its mouth open wide. "What is that?"

"That is a cat. *Our* cat."

"That thing looks like it has all kinds of diseases," Ashley said. "And it looks like it would eat my face in my sleep."

Theresa looked at her screen. "His name is Bananas, and you will show my child some respect."

"You can't be serious."

Theresa shoved the screen in front of Ashley's face. "How can you say no to Bananas?"

"Easy," said Ashley. "No."

With a heavy, exaggerated sigh, Theresa put the phone away. "Fine. I'll find another one."

Ashley felt the sinking suspicion that she's been had. "This was your negotiation strategy all along, wasn't it?"

Fighting back a grin, Theresa said, "I don't have any idea what you're talking about."

MADISON ADJUSTED her lens as she aimed her camera at the sparkling statuesque beauty at the front of the room. She snapped several shots of the children settling in on the floor watching with rapt attention as the woman sat in a tiny chair and displayed the books she'd be reading to them that day.

Vivian was a natural with children. She was bold and animated and knew exactly how to own a room while also inviting the littles to share the spotlight with her whenever they got the urge to shine. After capturing the attention and hearts of the packed little room with the beautifuly affirming story, *I Am Enough*, Vivian whipped them into a swirling, squealing frenzy with *Just Add Glitter*.

The kids were completely smitten with Vivian's asymmetrical red bob and sparkly blue satin wrap dress. She always said glitter and sparkles were better than any swaying gold watch for hypnotizing little ones, but Madison knew it was way more than that. In or out of drag, Vivian was mesmerizing. Her smooth, rich voice had soothed Madison's nerves on many occasions. Particularly over the past year.

As Vivian wrapped up the show and the librarians opened the door into the adjoining craft room for a glitter extravaganza, the crowd erupted into a roar of applause while the children lined up to thank Vivian. Madison captured a particularly adorable shot of a tiny child who couldn't have been more than three, reaching up to gently touch one of Vivian's chandelier earrings. Madison understood the urge completely. Every time she saw those beauties she wished she had a special occasion to borrow them for. Or even the courage to wear them.

She snapped another photo of Vivian laughing—a gorgeous full-body laugh—surrounded by giggling children as parents took their hands, thanked Viv, and shuffled out of the meeting room. Madison loved taking these photos, and she was especially grateful for the pleasant distraction going into this weekend.

Photographing the Drag Queen Story Times had started as a favor to Viv, and turned into a regular volunteer gig for the library. She loved photographing the children's events. Even though she didn't really interact with them, she loved being kid adjacent, experiencing their wonder and joy through the lens. It filled any tiny recesses of her soul that might have an inkling of an urge to have a family of her own one day. Madison didn't have the time or patience for raising children. Certainly not alone, but mostly not at all.

Heck, she couldn't even handle a dog, how would she fit a *child* into her life?

Better to keep things simple. Streamlined. That most certainly meant kid-free.

"Another success," said Madison. "As fabulous as your contouring, as always."

"Of course." Viv slipped a hand around Madison's arm and pointed a long, meticulously manicured finger tipped with gold sparkles at Madison's camera. "Now, let's put that thing in its bag so you can buy me a coffee."

When not performing, Viv went by Doug and worked at the top marketing firm in the city. She still made a regular habit of mooching free coffees off of Madison but paid her back in fierce friendship, ceaseless joy, and the occasional fancy dinner.

"Can't," she said. "I need to get back to meet Ashley at the apartment."

Viv leaned back to give her a good long look with a raised eyebrow. "Ashley?"

"My dog walker. Trainer. Person," she stumbled. "For Bacchus."

Viv swatted her arm lightly and gave a knowing grin. "So she's 'Ashley' now, huh?"

"Since that's her name, yes."

With an exasperated sigh, Vivian removed her hand from Madison's arm so she could pack her camera freely. "Fine. Ashley it is then." She drug out the first syllable of the name like there was some illicit secret hidden within those letters. "How's that beast doing with Miss Ashley anyway?"

It was no secret that neither Vivian nor Doug were Bacchus's biggest fan. Doug wasn't fond of dogs to begin with, thanks to a less than pleasant childhood in rural Louisiana growing up with an uncle who raised fighting dogs, but he'd tried to give Bacchus the benefit of the doubt. For Callie. Doug would have done anything, faced down any monster for Callie, who he'd known since grade school. Their love for Callie was the biggest thing Doug and Madison had in common. The thing that brought them even closer after they lost Callie exactly a year ago tomorrow.

"Bacchus, believe it or not, is becoming quite the furry gentleman."

With a quick glance around to make sure there weren't any little lingering ears, Vivian wagged her eyebrows and said, "Furry gentleman, huh? Not sure if I want to use that in my profile or search for it."

Madison rolled her eyes and zipped the camera case shut before slinging it over her shoulder. "You wouldn't know what to do with a gentleman—furry or not—if I wrapped one up and had him delivered to you." She gave a teasing grin. "How's Troy, by the way?"

Doug and his husband, Troy, were regulars at Madison's house, but she hadn't seen them much lately. Of her own fault, of course, since hermitting had become a full-blown way of life this past year.

"Troy is doing great, thanks for asking." Viv tapped a finger to her full, coral, pouty lips. "Hmm, this could be a business plan, M." She flashed her hands in the air to mimic a billboard or flashing sign. "Furry Gentleman Delivery Service."

"This is New Orleans, Viv. Pretty sure someone's probably already beaten you to that pitch."

With a grunt, Vivian followed Madison out of the library. "True. I'll just have to come up with some other genius plan. That dog person thinking of expanding? I need a new pet project." She giggled. "*Pet*. Get it?"

"Yes, I get it," Madison groaned. "And no, as amazing as Ashley is with Bacchus, I don't get the impression that this is an intended career path for her."

"The amazing Ashley, huh?"

"Stop it."

"What?" Vivian shrugged and waved goodbye to the security guard as they walked through the automatic sliding doors and out into the bright sunshine and crisp December air. The temperature had dropped a solid ten degrees while they were inside the library. "You said it."

"Stop trying to make this something it isn't."

"Well, what is it then?"

Madison considered the answer carefully, so as not to add

more fuel to Viv's gossip-fire. "She's my dog trainer and dog walker. That's it."

Vivian bent her head and with a throaty whisper asked, "Is she cute?"

"I'm not answering that," Madison said, trying to wipe the image from her mind of Ashley's bright smile and her adorable legs in those festive penguins-in-Santa-hats fleece leggings when she showed up to walk Bacchus yesterday.

"You're not answering 'cause she's cute. I see how it is."

"I'm not answering because she's my *employee*." Madison's phone dinged in her back pocket. She pulled it out and quickly scanned the email snippet on the lock screen. Excitement vibrated through her. She'd been waiting for a response exactly like this for weeks. Months. But an unexpected and overwhelming wave of anxiety hit her as she put the phone back in her pocket. "Maybe not for long, though."

"Uh-oh," Vivian said. "Did you nanny-cam her or something?"

Madison shook her head. "Nothing like that. Someone wants Bacchus."

Viv's eyes grew wide. "That's great. Finally!"

"Great. Yeah."

Viv made a grunt. "But when Bacchus goes, so does Miss Ashley trainer person." Madison opened her mouth to protest, but Viv cut her off. "There is no sense denying anything. But we don't have to talk about it right now if you don't want to."

"Thank you." Viv had been Madison's rock this past year. She had no idea how she would have gotten through a day of it without Viv in her corner.

In an uncharacteristic moment of hesitation, Viv bit her bright bottom lip then said, "What do you think about expanding tomorrow evening? We could invite a couple of people over besides just me and Troy. I'm sure others would love to be there and support you and toast to Callie along with us."

Madison's heart clenched at the thought of being around other people during her misery. She couldn't possibly.

But she also knew she couldn't go through it alone. And that she wasn't the best at making decisions when she was emotional.

She reached her car in the parking lot and turned to Viv. "I'll think about."

"Good." Vivian narrowed her dark eyes and pointed a finger at Madison. "You'd better."

"Promise." She tiptoed to kiss Viv on the cheek.

Vivian relaxed and returned the kiss. "Fair enough. But I'm gonna hold you to that." She winked and took a step backward onto the curb. "Don't want to keep The Amazing Ashley waiting."

Madison ignored the dig and closed herself in the car, waving goodbye to Vivian. While the car warmed up, she did her best *not* to think about the Amazing Ashley or how the last thing she should have been thinking about on this particular weekend was some other woman's penguin leggings.

CHAPTER 5

Madison stared at the email on her computer screen. It was an email she'd been waiting to magically appear in her inbox for almost a year, so she didn't quite understand the pit of sorrow and panic that had opened in her stomach at the sight of those words.

She leaned back in her desk chair and considered her reply. Not stalling. No. And definitely not reconsidering.

She closed her eyes and focused on her breath while Pete Fountain's clarinet runs filled the living room of her tiny home. Her thinking music. Pete Fountain always reminded her of her dad, how he was always listening to Pete's albums, and how he'd taken her to watch him and his band play a couple times when she was little. Back when she still believed things were meant to last. Before she lost him and, later, Callie.

Bacchus placed his head on her thigh, looking up at her with those bright, all-knowing eyes of his. Like he could see through Madison the same way his original person had been able to see right through her.

A horrifying alert blared from her phone, causing

Madison to jump in her chair and Bacchus to bark in circles. "Hush," she commanded, just like Ashley had instructed her earlier in the week. To her complete shock, Bacchus stopped barking and looked to her for further instruction.

It had to be a fluke.

A light, rhythmic knock sounded on the door. But not just any rhythm. Jingle Bells.

Madison opened the door, and Ashley's eager face lit up the entryway.

"Hey." Her voice was as bright as her enthusiasm and almost as bright as the festively cheery green and pink striped long-sleeved T-shirt she wore. She held up a narrow blue binder. "I have a list of new tricks to look through. I organized them by difficulty level. If you want to you can help me decide what to work on next with him. I figured, since you have to live with him, you should have some input on what you'd like him to learn. We still need to work on distractions and that bolting instinct, but some fun tricks at home will help keep his mind busy so he isn't so antsy when he does go out."

A ping of guilt stabbed at Madison's gut as she thought about that email reply she'd just sent.

As much as Madison needed a clean slate from this dog and her memories of the woman who'd brought him into her life, she'd grown fond of Bacchus and Ashley's contagious enthusiasm filling her home every day. Their bond was so pure and vibrant, she hated that she'd be tearing them apart. But Ashley deserved the truth. Sooner rather than later.

"Right," she said. "That makes sense. I'll take a look at it in a minute."

Ashley set the binder on the table but wrinkled her brow when she turned back to face Madison. "Everything okay? Did he eat something again?"

"No, no. Everything's fine," she assured Ashley. Doing her best to muster up some cheer. And maybe hide her guilt. "All my shoes are safe."

She had to admit Ashley had done a fantastic job so far. Whatever she'd done with Bacchus, he'd completely abandoned his habit of chewing on everything that belonged to Madison.

Ashley's face glowed with pride. "Oh! I almost forgot." She plopped her gigantic canvas purse on the table beside the binder and dug around inside it. "I have a present for the best boy in the world."

After a sly grin at Madison, she lowered her eyes to Bacchus, who was sitting in his perfectly trained position at her feet, looking up expectantly at her. It was almost adorable. Too adorable. Reminding her of Callie and a much tinier puppy, but also reminding her of all the potential memories of Callie and Bacchus that were stolen from her.

Madison couldn't stand another moment of silence with her thoughts. "What is it?" She laughed. "I think he's got more self-control than I do now."

Ashley pulled her hand from behind her back and held out a thick collar with festive pink stripes and bright green trees. "Someone needed a bit of cheer to make him even more snazzy than he already is."

She froze, as if remembering something, and took a slow, terrified look around the apartment.

"Unless you don't celebrate Christmas. Or any holidays." Ashley bit her lip and looked up at Madison, her big blue eyes filled with regret. "Oh crap, I messed up, didn't I? I'm sorry." She stuffed it back in her bag. Words flew out of her mouth at a dizzying pace. "I can return it. Or exchange it. I think I saw one with skulls. Or birds? I don't know why birds. That's weird, right? But I have the receipt!"

"Ashley." Madison held up a hand to stop the avalanche of explanations and apologies. She held her palm in front of her until Ashley closed her mouth and started breathing again. "It's fine. I promise."

She glanced around the admittedly bleak-looking room with the shades still drawn and felt a little embarrassed. She knew she didn't owe anyone an explanation or a list of reasons why she wasn't decorating her house for the holidays, but Ashley's kindness and hard work—the closest thing Madison had experienced to friendship from anyone besides Doug and Troy in a long time—over the last couple weeks deserved...*something*. An answer, at least.

"I'm just not that into the holidays." She almost said, "this year" but that would be a lie. She'd never really been a holly jolly kind of person. That had been Callie's role. But she had to admit, the collar was adorable. "The collar looks really cute on him."

"Well, I have enough holiday cheer for all of us." Ashley smiled and gave Bacchus a good petting while she replaced his old collar with the new one. "There. Now you're extra handsome." She booped his nose with her own, and he licked her in response. It was just about the cutest thing Madison had ever seen.

Normally, she might find someone as perky as Ashley kind of annoying. But perky wasn't exactly the right word for Ashley. Enthusiastic? Exuberant? All of the 'E' words. Definitely.

On Ashley, all of those things seemed so right. Her excitement was never forced or for show. She wasn't trying to impress anyone, not even Madison. She just...was. And as much as Madison had grown to resent that big bundle of fur over the last year, her heart warmed at the sight of Ashley loving on Bacchus. He deserved someone who loved him that much.

Her phone rang, and Madison looked down at the number flashing on the screen. It wasn't in her contacts, but she recognized it from the email she'd received earlier. The potential adopter.

When she looked up, the scene between Ashley and Bacchus no longer warmed her heart. It crushed it beneath brewing guilt and a year of growing desperation.

"I have to take this," she said, holding up her phone.

"No problem. I have to take *this*." Ashley grabbed Bacchus's leash and lifted it. She giggled, and damn it if Madison didn't giggle back.

Madison.

Giggled.

What the hell was going on here?

"Be safe out there," she called out. "No one around here knows how to drive in this weather."

Ashley flashed a thumbs up and a brilliant smile before she closed the front door behind them, leaving Madison alone with a ringing phone and a task she really wished she could avoid.

ASHLEY GRABBED A PARTICULARLY large pile of poop with the inverted plastic bag in her hand, a parting gift for the citizens of the Lower Garden District from a snazzily decked out Border Collie. The pile nearly froze the moment it hit the sidewalk, which Ashley supposed she should be grateful for. Nothing was worse than a hot, steamy mid-August sidewalk turd; however, she had a hard time feeling thankful while she was shivering under her layers *and* her thick coat.

The temperature had dropped another five degrees since they'd started their walk and, according to her weather app, it had dipped below freezing ahead of schedule. But Ashley had still guided Bacchus down one extra block than usual before they turned the corner to circle back home. She knew Madison wouldn't want to take him out farther than the tiny patch of grass in front of her house later that night, and it would be too cold and the sidewalks and roads too icy for Ashley to come back out here to give him an evening walk, so she made sure to get a good, long afternoon trip around the neighborhood to work out plenty of energy.

Her hands shook as she tied a knot in the bag and headed back toward Madison's house. Normally, Bacchus would make a strong case for another jog around the block or to go a little farther, but with their extra block and the mist of light, freezing rain now falling on them, even Bacchus was ready to go home. And as much as Ashley loved hanging out with this dog, knowing that Madison's delightful little giggle was back in that house made Ashley eager to return there too.

Halfway back to the house, tires screeched behind them, and Ashley turned to see a gigantic gray sedan skidding out of control. She yanked Bacchus's leash to pull him back while he barked frantically at the car aiming straight for them.

Ashley's breath caught in her chest, and the sounds of the city evaporated. All she could hear was Bacchus, whose barking now sounded like it was muffled by the roaring in her head. Another screech and the car spun sideways, jumping the curb a few yards from them and crashing through a wrought iron fence and into the front porch of a duplex with a thunderous bang.

Ashley stood frozen, staring at the now steaming car and the driver slumped over the wheel, confused but conscious.

People rushed out of nearby homes and flocked to the car. A moment later, a woman held Ashley's arm, cradling her elbow gently and staring into Ashley's eyes.

"Are you all right? Here, sit." The woman gestured at the curb nearby. She had long wavy brown hair streaked with gray and wide gray eyes to match. She looked like she was the one who needed to sit down. Everyone around them looked that way. Shocked. Terrified.

"I'm fine."

Was she?

Bacchus barked ferociously at the car, and everything came into focus. The ice. The car. The bricks on the ground. Several people on their phones nearby. A nurse identifying himself to the driver as he crouched beside the man. The five yards of space between Ashley and a trip in an ambulance. Christmas in the hospital. At best.

"Are you sure? You look like you're in shock. Here, you should sit," she insisted again.

"Really, I'm fine."

"And your dog?"

"He's not…" Ashley looked down at Bacchus who had stopped barking and was now licking her hand, willing her with his tongue to make sense of everything. "He's okay. We weren't hurt. Just…lucky."

"Someone's looking out for you today." The woman patted Ashley on the shoulder. "Looks like you've got yourself a guardian angel."

Ashley had never been religious. Even when her parents brought her to church as a kid, she never really felt a connection to any of her church's teachings. The idea that love was only for some didn't sit well with her, even before they made it clear she was a "sinner" and no longer welcome there.

"Maybe a Christmas elf," she suggested instead.

The woman laughed. It was warm and jolly. As a holiday season laugh should be. But this wasn't some fluffy movie. She'd been nearly run over a second ago. Why were they laughing again?

"I like the sound of that." The woman waved at Bacchus. "Well, take care getting home. I don't know how many good deeds Christmas elves are allotted in one day."

The woman walked away and Ashley gathered her wits in time to shout, "Thank you," at her back.

She stood there for a few more minutes with Bacchus eventually lying on the cement beside her. She told herself she was waiting for the ambulance to arrive for the driver, but she wasn't sure her wobbly legs could carry her very far. They still felt like they weren't entirely attached to the rest of her body, although she no longer felt like she might pass out or throw up.

She was cold, but appropriately cold now, not awash in physical shock. She just wasn't sure she could make it more than a few steps, much less the remaining block to Madison's house.

"Ashley?"

She turned her head toward the sound of her name. The direction in which she should have been walking. The direction in which Madison now hurried toward her down the sidewalk. As she got closer, Madison's eyes widened, registering Ashley's complete silence and her unresponsive body language.

Madison now sprinted toward Ashley and the nearby crash scene, the ambulance lights flashing in the background. Kind of pretty. Almost like flashing Christmas lights. Madison's long, dark blonde hair bounced around her face and shoulders until she stopped just in front of Ashley and put her hands on the sides of Ashley's arms.

"Are you okay?"

Bacchus sat then stood and sat then stood like his motor was on repeat. He didn't know what to do, but his excitement at seeing Madison was clear. Even if she didn't notice him.

Ashley nodded. "We were…right here. The whole time. The car didn't hit us."

She took Ashley's face in her icy hands and stared into Ashley's eyes. Ashley felt a whole new dizzying head rush, but this time she couldn't blame adrenaline or shock or fear.

Well, maybe a little fear.

Madison's light brown eyes stared into her, fixated on her pupils, and Ashley felt herself wobbling on her still-frozen-in-place legs. Madison's hands on her face seemed to hold her entire body upright though.

"You don't look good." Madison shook her head and stumbled over her words. "I mean, you do. Look good. Fine, I mean. Except…" She took a deep breath and centered herself. She removed her palms from the sides of Ashley's face, leaving Ashley's skin exposed to the wind and craving that contact back. "I heard the commotion and called your cell. When you didn't answer I walked outside and saw all the flashing lights and saw a jumble of traffic and…"

Her voice trembled slightly as it trailed off. Ashley had never even heard her phone ring. "I'm sorry. I didn't mean to worry you like that. Bacchus is fine."

Madison finally looked down at Bacchus. She looked back up at Ashley and smiled appreciatively. "He was in good hands." Madison's face sank again. "Are you sure you aren't in shock or something?"

Ashley glanced over her shoulder as the emergency responders helped the driver into the ambulance. "Honestly?" She turned back to Madison. "I can't move. I tried to walk Bacchus home, but I couldn't make my legs move. I was afraid I might fall over."

Madison slipped a hand around Ashley's free arm, on the other side of Bacchus. Madison's hand on her arm warmed Ashley all the way down to her toes. It was then that she realized Madison wasn't wearing a coat and must have been frozen worse than Ashley's feet to the pavement.

"I won't let you fall," Madison said. "I promise."

CHAPTER 6

Once they were back inside the house after that cold, silent walk, Madison removed her coat and mustered a calm, steady voice. "Would you prefer tea or hot chocolate? Or something stronger?"

"Neither, thank you. I should head out now before the roads get worse."

"Oh no." Madison shook her head emphatically, while she leaned her hands against the back of the nearby couch so Ashley wouldn't see them shaking. "You're not getting on those roads. The city officials have already made their statement. No driving, except emergency vehicles."

Every time it dipped below freezing with even a tiny amount of moisture, the entire city shut down. Growing up in Connecticut, Madison used to love snow days as a kid. Her family moved to Metairie when she was a teenager and quickly learned that hurricane days and ice days weren't nearly as fun. Necessary, since they didn't have salt trucks around here, but not at all what she'd call fun.

The aftermath though…she could get some gorgeous photos after an ice storm. She had an entire folder on her backup drive filled with beautiful photos of the city after an ice storm last January. They were black and white, like all of her photos from those months, and the stark contrast only highlighted the beauty of those crystal formations hanging from all of that fabulous architecture.

"And the streetcars and buses aren't running either, so don't get any ideas."

Madison patted the couch. She wanted to grab hold of Ashley and physically guide her to sit on the cushion just like she'd held her arm and guided her all the way home. Her brain tried to convince her they were safe inside now, and Ashley did seem much more steady on her feet after a block of walking and leaning against Madison.

But some part other than her brain didn't want to let go. She liked holding Ashley close. And she'd been terrified when she'd seen Ashley standing there amid that chaos. Terrified wasn't even the right word. Not when her brain was also flashing images of Callie from the morgue on a similarly icy night. "You're staying here for dinner."

"But the temps will just drop lower," Ashley protested. But she took a seat on the couch anyway, still seeming a bit shaky. At least emotionally. "The roads won't melt until tomorrow morning."

"I have a guest room you can stay in. I'm sure Bacchus would love a sleepover."

Ashley's mood visibly lifted at that, and her eyes glinted with amusement. "Thanks. I appreciate it. But I don't want to—"

"Not up for debate." Madison gave a curt nod with a tight smile. "It's the least I can do for all the help you've been with Bacchus."

"I had a good student," she said. "And you *are* paying me, after all."

"Look at this dog." Bacchus's ears perked up when she pointed at him lying on the floor beside the couch, perfectly content near Ashley's feet. "I can't ever repay you enough for this."

Ashley blushed a little. "He's a good student, really. I think he mostly liked giving you a hard time."

It had been a joke, and Ashley's tone confirmed it, but Madison had always wondered if he blamed her for losing his *real* person. He'd been so young when Callie died, and he'd only been with them a few weeks, so she doubted he even remembered her after a month or so passed. But Madison still wondered if that's why he'd been so willful and mischievous with her. She blamed herself, so why wouldn't he blame her too? And Madison knew how poor a substitute she must be for Callie.

"I think he just likes you." Madison grinned and before she could stop herself added, "Can't blame him."

She shouldn't have said that. She shouldn't have even *thought* that. Not this weekend. And especially not while Ashley was still pale and stiff and visibly shaken from the near-accident just a few minutes ago.

They both sat frozen, staring at each other across the room, neither sure what to say next. Madison hated seeing this indomitable force of a woman so unsettled. So speech-less. So afraid.

But she knew exactly what might cheer her up. She held up one finger. "Hang on a second."

Ashley, confused, gave a hesitant, "Okay," then leaned against the couch cushions while Madison jumped to her feet.

She made a beeline for her bedroom closet, flung open the door, and stood on her tiptoes to shuffle the boxes on the upper shelf. After a brief game of box Jenga, she managed to slide out the correct plastic storage container. She returned to the living room and tried to hide the smug satisfaction bubbling inside her.

She placed the box on the coffee table and made a flourish with her hands. "Ta-da!"

"What is it?" Ashley looked even more confused than ever. More confused than she'd been at Madison's previous implication that Ashley was irresistibly likable.

"Open it."

Ashley snapped open the lid, and her eyes widened as she peered inside. She looked up at Madison, her eyes glittering with excitement and hope. "Really? Are you sure?"

Madison nodded. "You were right. This place could use some cheering up. And this," she gestured out the window, "and you being stuck here feels like a sign."

A wide smile stretched across Ashley's face as she reached in and held up a piece of shiny silver tinsel. "If you're sure. I don't want to overstep, and when I asked before I didn't know—"

"No, it's fine. I mean it. You were right and this place is depressing. I have a right to be sad, but I don't have to live in a place that *looks* sad." Truthfully, the last thing Callie would have wanted was her living like this, especially a whole year later. Bringing some light into her space suddenly felt like the perfect way to honor Callie's memory. Especially this weekend, on the anniversary of losing her. Madison shrugged. "Who knows. Maybe I'll even go wild and get a tree later. Maybe I'll get a Christmas Eve tree like we used to do when I was little."

"Normally I would fully support good tree intentions, but in this case, maybe not."

Madison looked around, then tilted her head at Ashley. "Too much? Living room too small?" She'd never tried to fit a full-sized tree in here before, only tabletop ones, but she always figured she could move things around and squeeze one in.

Ashley nodded at the snoring dog near her feet. "Too much puppy still."

She'd been hoping to avoid this conversation for as long as possible, but she didn't want to spring this on Ashley at the last minute. And it seemed like something Ashley would need to prepare herself for. Madison had never counted on them building this kind of connection so quickly, but here they were. And Ashley deserved the truth.

Her stomach sank as she looked down at Bacchus, then back up at Ashley, who was now thoroughly delighted by the prospect of decorating. Madison just couldn't bring herself to extinguish that joy and have that smile disappear again.

Later.

Ashley was now stuck here for the night. There would be plenty of time to tell her the truth later.

ASHLEY BALANCED on a dining chair in the living room while she held a string of lights up against the wall. Stevie Wonder and Andra Day filled the little house with the joy of Christmas. It was practically perfect, exactly what Ashley had been missing this holiday season.

Almost perfect enough to make her forget that she'd almost died on the sidewalk less than an hour ago.

Almost.

Madison fumbled in a kitchen junk drawer for more wall hooks, making so much noise Ashley wondered what she could possibly have crammed in that drawer. The otherwise neat, tidy, and in control Madison didn't allow a single speck of disarray to enter her apartment, so Ashley liked imagining that she shoved all of her chaos and disorganization into that one junk drawer.

She wondered if she had an internal drawer for emotional clutter too. It seemed like a kind of superpower to Ashley. Not necessarily one she was envious of, but one she was sure other people must wish she had. As much as she had a clear focus when it came to her ambitions and career, she couldn't contain the rest of her life that way. Which was mostly why there *wasn't* much to call the rest of her life.

Madison rounded the corner waving a packet of clear plastic wall hooks. "Found them," she sang in a cheery tone. Madison dug inside the open package and handed a hook to Ashley. She stuck it to the wall and looped the end of the light string over it. "Perfect."

At first, Madison's enthusiasm for decorating had seemed forced. She was clearly decking her halls as a gift to Ashley and maybe a little guilt over Ashley's near-death experience while walking Bacchus. But with every item they hung, Madison's delight visibly multiplied.

Madison dug through the rest of the box contents. "Not much left to work with."

Ashley grabbed a couple of cute deer figurines and some greenery. "How about these on the bookshelves?"

They'd agreed to not put out anything Bacchus-height or below. That meant no displays on the coffee or end tables.

"Good call." Madison placed a hand on Ashley's shoulder. "How about I start some dinner, while you finish this up?"

That hand on her shoulder rendered Ashley frozen and speechless. Her brain scrambled for ways to keep it there, then ran through plans for how to get Madison's hands on other parts of her body. "I can help you with dinner."

With a squeeze of her shoulder, Madison said, "You can

help me when you're done here. I'll get things started." Then, she removed her hand and gave a warm, inviting smile as she left the room.

Ashley watched her from behind until she disappeared into the kitchen. Her shoulder was still warm from Madison's touch, and she didn't want to move, fearing that sensation would fade away. She looked down at the deer in her hands and broke out in a full grin.

She shouldn't be this excited about the thought of making dinner with Madison. And she *certainly* shouldn't be this excited about Madison's touch. She'd gotten plenty of flack from Theresa when she'd called to let her know she was stuck at Madison's for the night and had tried to reassure her roommate that it didn't mean anything more than an early ice storm had trapped her. If Theresa knew about those tingles from a simple arm touch, Ashley would never hear the end of it.

WHEN ASHLEY JOINED Madison in the kitchen later, she found her stirring a pan of sauce with a pot boiling beside her. She had on a short black apron with a gold fleur-de-lis pattern over her black T-shirt and maroon sweatpants. Because of course Madison wore an apron to cook. It was downright adorable.

"Reporting for dinner duty," Ashley said cheerfully. "What can I help with?"

Madison nodded toward the pot while she continued to stir. "Toss the pasta in the water."

Ashley opened the box of spaghetti and dumped it into the boiling water. While she grabbed a big spoon from a nearby crock and stirred the pasta to separate it, she took a sniff of the aroma wafting up from that sauce. "Oh my gosh, did you make that in like fifteen minutes?"

"Not exactly." She pointed the wooden spoon over her shoulder. "Freezer. I like to make a big pot and freeze portions for just this sort of emergency."

"Because everyone has iced in guests on the regular around here?"

Madison laughed. "With the drainage in this area? Substitute flooded in for iced in and that sounds about right."

"So you have friends over a lot?" She and Theresa rarely had friends over. They frequently met people out for dinners or drinks or whatever, but when they came home it was usually to crash, not host and entertain. Ashley shook her head and nervously dunked the spoon back in the water to stir the pasta again. "I'm sorry. Ignore me. That's none of my business."

She was doing it again. Asking questions like this woman wasn't her boss.

"It's fine," Madison said. "It's a friendly question, and we're friends, right?"

Ashley froze as tingles made their way up the back of her neck. *Friends.* "Sure. I mean, I don't know?" *Yes, please.*

Madison glanced sideways and gave a reassuring grin. "I hope so."

Heat flowed through her entire body, and she was glad for the steam rising off the pot to explain the flush her cheeks surely had. "I'd like that."

"Me too." Madison looked back at her sauce. "And the answer is that I used to. But not for a long time. I have one good friend who comes over pretty regularly, sometimes with his husband. I used to host a dinner or cocktail gathering most weeks." Her expression changed drastically as sadness found its way into her eyes. "I haven't managed anything like that this year."

"Because of Bacchus?"

Madison hesitated. "In part." She looked at the dog curled up in his bed in the next room. "But honestly, even at his worst, he isn't the main reason."

"Why then?" Dang it. She was nosy to the core. "Sorry. Again. I just mean, you seemed sad when you said you don't have those gatherings anymore, so it doesn't make sense to stop doing something you enjoy." For Ashley, on the other hand, it made perfect sense. Having people over sounded exhausting. Cleaning and tidying before they came. Planning, making lists, shopping, and prepping food. Cleaning and tidying *again* after they left. She didn't have the time or energy for all of that.

But Madison seemed like she was totally in her element. And honestly, to Ashley's surprise, prepping dinner with Madison didn't feel at all like a chore. It felt warm and cozy, like a giant mug of hot chocolate for her soul. Like something she didn't even know she was missing.

Then, the realization hit her.

Unlike Ashley, Madison knew exactly what she was missing.

"Oh, crap, I'm so, so sorry," Ashley explained. "I completely forgot for a minute. And you said the holidays were hard and this year has been hard and—"

"It's okay," Madison said firmly. "Really, it's fine. I don't expect everyone to remember my sad story all the time."

"But I should have. And I shouldn't have pried."

"You didn't pry. You asked. Because that's what friends do." Madison gave a reassuring smile, but in that smile rested a hint of sadness that hadn't been there before Ashley'd begun her interrogation.

"Do you mind if I ask how long you two were together?"

"She lived with me here for about eight months before she died. Car accident. It was just a quick visit with her mom, and I stayed here because I had a wedding booked already." Madison forced an awkward smile laced with sadness as she paused her stirring and looked at Ashley. "You would have liked her. I think Callie loved Christmas almost as much as you do."

"Whoa, is that possible?" Ashley hoped the joke came off as lighthearted and supportive.

Madison chuckled a little. "We met a couple years ago. Well, more than that, if you count all the times I sat in her section at the little sandwich shop she worked at in the Warehouse District." Madison's eyes lit up at the memories, and Ashley couldn't help feel her own mood lifting. She found herself wishing she'd known the person who could have made Madison so happy. "I'd go out of my way after photo shoots to stop by for lunch when she was working. Then, I'd spend the afternoon inspired by seeing her, and I'd take photos around the neighborhood."

"She sounds wonderful."

"She was. I used to call her my muse." Madison laughed again. "She hated that. Always said I was my own muse, and I shouldn't ever let anyone take that away from me."

"Wow. That's some powerful stuff."

"She was right. Always." Madison sighed. "And you were right about it not making sense that I stopped doing something I used to enjoy. I do miss having gatherings here. And Callie would be furious with me for spending the entire last year shut up alone in the darkness like this."

"Well, it isn't dark in here anymore. And you aren't alone right now."

Madison looked over at the living room where lights

twinkled from the ceiling. Then, she looked back at Ashley, a twinkle in her eyes replacing the sadness now. "I'm really glad you're here."

Ashley felt her entire chest fill with butterflies. "The near-death stuff aside, I'm really glad too."

They stared at each other, lost in the moment and this strange new connection Ashley couldn't name but was fairly certain wasn't solely friendship. She'd never stared at Theresa like this in front of their stove. She couldn't remember ever staring at anyone like this that she didn't end up kissing. With perfect clarity, Ashley realized how much she wanted to kiss Madison right now.

She felt her body floating inch by inch toward her. The distance closed between them and Ashley's heart raced until the pasta sauce began making little bubbly explosions on its surface and the timer for the pasta went off.

Madison flinched and shut off the timer in a clumsy, hectic flurry of motions. When she turned back, Ashley could tell something had shifted.

"What's wrong?"

Madison hesitated. She opened and closed her mouth. Then she said. "It's about the tree."

"The tree? What tree?"

"Remember how I was talking about getting a tree Christmas Eve?"

Ashley nodded, confused but following the explanation so far.

Madison hesitated again, then said, "Bacchus may not be here for Christmas."

No longer following the explanation and utterly lost, Ashley asked, "Why? Is he staying with someone else?"

"No." Madison looked away, staring at the pot and the pasta overcooking beneath the surface of the starchy water.

"Is everything okay?" Ashley struggled to remain calm. She'd grown so fond of that dog and its owner, she couldn't bear the thought of something happening to either of them. "Does he need to stay at the vet or something?"

Madison looked back at Ashley, her eyes rimmed red now. "That phone call I got earlier. It was about Bacchus. I found someone to adopt him."

CHAPTER 7

Ashley's head felt like a loosely tethered balloon, floating and wobbling as Madison spoke. She tried to focus on the words coming out of Madison's mouth, but she couldn't hear anything but that one sentence on repeat.

I found someone to adopt him.

"But...I thought..." She swallowed the lump in her throat. "Has he been misbehaving again?"

Madison shook her head insistently. "No, no, of course not. You've done a wonderful job with him. You really have. Which is why this is going to work out this time."

Work out.

Ashley had thought things already *were* working out. Bacchus was the perfect furry gentleman now. Well, mostly. He was definitely in better shape than when she'd started this job. She knew that. So what had gone wrong?

"I...I don't understand," she said.

Madison pressed her lips together and took a deep breath. She looked down at Bacchus, then back up at Ashley. Her dark eyes were sad and regretful. "It's just...hard. For me. I see him, and I see...her."

"Oh. Right."

Of course. Her. Callie. Of course, Bacchus reminded Madison of her. Especially this time of year.

"I know you've grown attached to him, but…" Madison paused and took another deep breath, this time her eyes focused on Ashley's. "This was always the plan."

"The plan," Ashley repeated. "Right. Sure."

The sauce made another little bubbly explosion in the saucepan, and Madison reached to turn the burner off. Then she grabbed the sides of the stockpot holding the pasta water. "I'd better drain this before it's completely ruined."

"I'm going to just…um…run to the restroom before we eat."

Madison froze with both hands on the pot handles. Her voice soft and sad, she said, "Ashley, I—"

"No, no, I'm good. I'll be right back."

Ashley backed out of the kitchen, then darted down the hall to the bathroom. To process the news. To collect her thoughts. To wad up toilet paper and dab at the mascara running beneath her eyes.

Her emotions tended to run amok, out in the open for the whole world to see. When faced with something like the news that Madison was giving away Bacchus, there was no chance Ashley could hide her emotions. There was no magical mask she could pull up to hide her confusion, disbelief, sadness…her utter disappointment.

Her attachment to that dog had snuck up on her. She'd grown to love this job, and she'd pretty much stopped thinking of it as a job entirely. She knew he wasn't her dog, but they'd bonded almost immediately and she didn't think she could feel so heartbroken over the thought of saying goodbye to someone else's pet after such a short time.

Not to mention saying goodbye to his owner.

Ashley leaned against the counter as she felt herself growing dizzy with anxiety, no longer a result of the shock of the accident she'd witnessed.

The more Madison had spoken, the more she'd explained the sound logic beneath her decision, the more a hole had grown beneath Ashley in that kitchen, threatening to swallow her and her entire new life.

No Bacchus. No more Madison.

The two were a package deal, and losing one meant the other disappearing from her life as well. It had only been a couple weeks, but with multiple daily visits, Ashley already couldn't imagine her life without them. Bacchus's adoption meant losing more than a job. She would be losing a friend. And it wasn't like she had many of those in her life besides Theresa. Party pals, sure. But not real friends. Those weren't in the plan, and she'd kind of forgotten how important they were.

But that was part of the problem. Madison wasn't her friend. She was her employer. She shouldn't have been confusing the two in the first place.

Ashley threw out her tear-stained wad of toilet paper and stared at herself in the mirror. She took a deep breath, then left the bathroom to eat overcooked pasta, force out fake smiles, and pretend everything was fine.

To pretend as if she was prepared to face life without Bacchus and Madison.

MADISON INSISTED that Ashley didn't need to help clear the dishes, but Ashley wasn't having it. Ashley didn't strike Madison as the type to sit around while other people did anything in her presence. One of the few things they seemed to have in common.

Not that she was tallying things they had in common. No. That would be ridiculous.

After Madison handed her the last cleaned dish, Ashley wiped it with the towel and peered through the living room to the window. "Well, it looks like the weather's cleared up. I appreciate dinner so much. I should be able to head back now."

Madison shook her head emphatically. "No way. First, it's dark outside. You can't even see if it's raining from here. And second, it's even colder now which means there's no chance those roads have melted. Plan's the same. My guest room is ready and waiting for you."

"I'm sure it would be okay. I've driven in worse."

"I'm not worried about your driving," Madison said. "I'm worried about the rest of the idiots out there."

She'd worried about Callie driving last year too. The weather had been crappy, and Callie's mom lived out in the middle of nowhere in some hilly Northern Mississippi back-woods. But Callie had insisted it would be fine.

"I feel...weird, staying here." Ashley looked incredibly uncomfortable. Something that didn't look right on her. Sure, she was an anxious ball of overinflated emotions some-times, but she always kept a polished exterior. Or at least she used to. The more time they spent together and the more they'd gotten to know one another, the more that polished wall crumbled around Ashley. Madison didn't like seeing her worried, but she did appreciate the honesty and comfort growing between them.

Despite the bombshell news Madison had just dropped.

Ashley had clearly been upset by the news, but she'd handled it like she seemed to handle everything—with a dash of forced confidence. Madison, on the other hand, didn't possess such coping skills and had stumbled through their dinner conversations, trying desperately to keep her own emotions in check.

She wasn't sure what was upsetting her more: upsetting Ashley with the news or the inevitability that there wouldn't be a reason to see Ashley anymore. To talk to her. To sit next to her, so close she could smell that cherry blossom body spray she always wore.

"You're a friend. And the weather's bad," she said. "You're using my guest room. That's what the room is for. Nothing to feel weird about."

Except she knew the words were a lie even as they fell out of her mouth. Friend? Sure, she'd loved decorating and making dinner together. And she'd loved even more their conversations about how they each found their way to New Orleans and their families and their careers. The whole afternoon and evening had been exactly what Madison needed. Today, especially.

But those flutters she felt when they stood side by side at the stove or brushed hands cleaning the dishes...those weren't friend flutters. Madison hadn't felt those kinds of flutters since...well, in a very long time. And she wasn't sure she was ready to replace those with flutters from someone new.

She nodded toward the hall. "Come on. I'll show you where you can crash. By the time Bacchus needs a walk in the morning, the sun should be up and the forecast says the roads should be melted and safe again. Well, as safe as the roads around here get."

Ashley hesitated a moment, then thanked her and reluctantly followed Madison down the hall and through the first door on the left. The room was small but cozy. Callie had insisted it should look homey and inviting, and Madison hadn't touched a thing in here over the last year. Doug had slept in here a few nights, mostly during those first couple of months. He hadn't wanted to leave her alone, and she would always be grateful for those first few nights he stayed and held her hand while she cried herself to sleep.

"This is your *guest* room?" Ashley took in the poster bed with the fluffy white down comforter and the hanging French Quarter prints Callie had bought from a local artist right after they'd moved in together. "It's way nicer than my regular room. Even when my clothes aren't covering the bed and my shoes aren't sprawled across the floor."

"Thanks. But I assure you I had nothing to do with decorating. My skills do not include nice-ing things up, I promise. Dinner is my only even remotely domestic skill." She laughed a little. "I'll be right back."

A minute later, she returned from her linen closet with an extra pillow and a heavy blanket. She placed them on the bed beside where Ashley sat, her brow wrinkled and her eyes deep in contemplation as she stared at the floor. Madison had no idea what was troubling her, but it couldn't be good. And it certainly didn't look like it had anything to do with the sleeping accommodations.

"What's wrong?"

Silence stretched out for a few moments, then Ashley finally spoke. "Why did you hire me?" She looked up at Madison with confusion on her face and sadness in her eyes. "I mean, if you were going to get rid of him, why did you bother to hire a trainer?"

"Honestly?" Madison sighed and tucked her hair behind her ears. "I didn't think I'd find anyone to take him. He was too much for me, for a lot of reasons, but I didn't want to hand him over to just anyone. He deserves a good person.

Someone right for him. And I'd been looking for a while, but had begun to give up hope. That's why I hired you. I couldn't handle him myself anymore, so I knew I at least needed help while I looked for new owners. And having him trained would help his chances of winning someone over."

Ashley took a deep breath and nodded. "That sounds fair."

"I want what's best for him. I really do." She paused, then said, "I just didn't count on you two bonding like you have." The unspoken truth about their own growing bond hung silently in the air between them.

As if on cue, Bacchus ran into the room and leaped onto the bed to lie beside Ashley. She smiled and rubbed his belly.

Madison hated that she'd have to split them up. Earlier that evening, when she'd explained that the potential adopter couldn't take Bacchus until after Christmas, she'd asked if Ashley wanted to take him instead. It would have been a dream scenario for everyone, but Ashley had been clear that she couldn't have a dog in her apartment. Her landlord had a one-cat-only policy.

Ashley kept a hand on Bacchus and looked up at Madison, a hint of hope in her expression. "What if *you're* what's best for him?"

Madison scoffed. "Did you see the condition he was in under my watch?" She shook her head. "No, he's better with someone else. Someone with the skills to handle him. Someone who can love him the way he deserves. Someone who doesn't randomly cry when she looks at him."

She hadn't meant to go that deep, but it was the truth. And Ashley deserved the truth as much as Bacchus deserved good people to love him.

"What if..." Ashley hesitated, looked down at Bacchus, then looked back up at Madison. "What if you're meant to be with each other? What if he's here to help you heal?"

Doug had asked the same thing one drunken night back in February. Madison had thought the idea ridiculous back then also.

"Sometimes, I really wish that was true. But wishing doesn't make something real," she said. "And that's a lot of responsibility to lay on one dog."

Ashley scratched at his floppy ear. "He can handle it. Besides, it won't all be his responsibility anymore."

Madison felt this weird flutter in her stomach. "What do you mean?"

A grin spread wide across Ashley's face, and the mischief and determination held in that smile looked delicious on her. Madison barely fought the urge to lean in and grab her face and kiss her.

Barely.

"I mean Bacchus and I are a team now." She raised her chin. "I'm going to help him win you over. I'm going to help him make you see that you need him as much as he needs you."

Madison tried to hide the smile forming at the edges of her mouth. "You're going to need more than three weeks for that. And that's all you've got."

Ashley's eyes glinted. "Challenge accepted."

CHAPTER 8

Ashley scrolled down the home page, checking for errors, wonky design elements, and any last-minute tweaks she needed to make before she showed the final product to Madison. This morning before she'd left, she'd managed to convince Madison to let her revamp her business website as thanks for being so kind and for letting Ashley stay over during the ice storm. She'd been working all afternoon on the redesign, showcasing some of Madison's best photographs in a carousel on the homepage. It looked gorgeous, but it didn't feel like *enough*.

The colorful twinkling lights hanging from the wall behind her cast a cheerful rainbow glow onto the screen. After spending last night stuck at Madison's, she'd been on such a high and filled with so much nervous energy yesterday that she'd stopped at a store on her way home. She'd bought three more bags of decorations. Now every single corner of her and Theresa's tiny apartment was crammed with Christmas cheer.

Ashley had been obsessed with the whole holiday season for as long as she could remember. Ever since her parents split when she was a kid, she'd longed for a house filled with decorations, lights, music, and cookies. But neither of her parents had any interest in those things, and they weren't about to fake it just for her. No matter how much she begged those first few years bouncing back and forth between new parental apartments.

Once she got her own place, she made sure that every December was extra festive. Everything sparkled in celebration of all the good things that happened during the year.

But this year's decorations were over the top, even for her.

Ashley tried to refocus her attention on Madison's website, but she couldn't stop thinking that this wasn't enough to thank Madison for her kindness and…friendship. Yes, they were using that term now. Officially. They still had a working business arrangement, but they were also *friends* now.

The word filled Ashley with excitement and joy, but also an unexpected emptiness. She couldn't stop herself from wanting to stretch the parameters of their friendship just a bit more. But wants and reality were two different things.

She thought for a moment about her stay at Madison's little duplex apartment. What kind of gift could she give her? What kinds of things did Madison like? She did a mental walk-through of Madison's home, taking note of her books, items on display, the few wall hangings…

Then, it hit her.

She opened a new search window and quickly typed in the artist's name from the print hanging in Madison's guest room. It had captured her attention and lulled her to sleep that night. The artist portrayed the heart of the city in a way that made it feel alive and comforting—comforting even after

Ashley's ordeal on those very streets. The artist's vision of the city reminded Ashley of the way Madison's photographs in the living room had also captured New Orleans.

That print had settled into Ashley's mind so soundly that she'd asked Madison about it over breakfast. It turned out to have been purchased by Madison's ex...well, not an ex, exactly. Ashley wasn't sure what to call Callie. She couldn't force herself to call her a girlfriend, because that sounded so current. Which, in turn, made Ashley's growing affection for Madison feel even more out of line.

Theresa walked into the room crunching on a bag of popcorn. She plopped onto the sofa cushion beside Ashley and leaned to look at the screen just as Ashley added one of the prints to her shopping cart. "Ooh, that's gorgeous."

"It's for Madison. A Christmas present. And to thank her for...well, for everything." Ashley kept her gaze on the screen, but she could *feel* Theresa's judgmental eyes on her.

"Shouldn't you be looking for a new job or something, instead of a gift for the boss that's about to fire you?"

Great. She'd been trying—and failing miserably—all weekend to not obsess about how she would be losing Bacchus and Madison so soon.

"She isn't firing me," Ashley insisted. "The position is simply expiring."

"Call it what you want. It still means unemployed."

"Maybe."

Theresa leaned away to give a sideways look at Ashley. "What's this maybe? You said she has an adopter for this dog. What, are you gonna walk Madison instead?"

"Stop." Ashley swatted Theresa's arm. "I mean she isn't taking him for three weeks."

"Riiiiiiight. And?"

"And that gives me and Bacchus three weeks to convince Madison that she needs Bacchus as much as he needs her."

Theresa gave an unconvinced frown. "And exactly how do you plan on doing that? I mean, I know how *I* would do it. But how do *you* think you're gonna accomplish this monumental feat?"

"I...I don't know yet," said Ashley. "Tell me how you would make this work?"

"Oh no." Theresa closed her eyes and shook her head firmly. "No, no, no. I am not dragging you over to the dark side. You stick to winning her over with tricks and treats or whatever. Things you're good at. You can't pull off sinister."

"Hey, I can be sinister."

"No, you can't. And that's why everyone loves you. Stay pure."

Ashley sighed. She had a sinking feeling that tricks, treats, and pureness wouldn't get the job done. Not this time.

"Speaking of sinister," she said. "You didn't sneak a cat in here yet, did you?"

"Not yet." Theresa grinned. "Haven't found Mr. or Mrs. Right yet."

"Good." The last thing Ashley needed right now was a cat. Especially when she had a bad case of dog-on-the-brain.

"Don't worry. I'll find him or her. And you'll love it." Theresa patted Ashley's leg and stood up. "Gotta get to work. Want me to bring you back anything?"

"No, thanks. I'll probably be asleep before you get back. These early morning walks are getting to me."

Theresa gave a sympathetic smile and left to get dressed for her dinner shift at the restaurant, leaving Ashley alone in the living room again with nothing but thoughts of how to keep Bacchus. And Madison.

Theresa was right. She really should be getting another

job lined up for after Christmas. But she just couldn't bring herself to abandon hope for those two.

All her life, Ashley had wanted a dog of her own. All her friends who had dogs lived in beautiful families where nothing went wrong and they all stayed together and had cheerful holiday celebrations and hung out at parks and did fun family stuff all the time. She'd come to believe that dogs were magical creatures. They were the sticky family glue that bonded people together and made everyone happy.

She wasn't delusional, but she truly believed that Bacchus was good for Madison. She just had to find a way for him to stick around a little longer until Madison believed that too.

MADISON LEANED against the wall near the kitchen, sipping from her cranberry gin fizz cocktail. It had been Callie's favorite, so it was the drink of choice for everyone in the room this evening.

Doug and his husband, Troy, huddled close on one end of Madison's sofa, wearing bright, crisp dress shirts in complementary shades of blue. They were the most adorable couple. Playful and casual, but always meticulously styled when Troy wasn't in scrubs.

Two other friends, Lydia and Camille sat in armchairs nearby. Lydia was a trauma counselor. Callie had met her through her work as a volunteer for a local crisis center. She'd always been a regular at their dinner parties, and she was an absolutely lovely woman. Her date, Camille, was a new face since she and Lydia had only recently begun dating.

The living room glowed softly from a floor lamp and the strings of lights Madison and Ashley hung the previous evening during the ice storm. As terrifying as that afternoon had been, Madison was grateful Ashley had helped decorate the place. She couldn't bring herself to do it alone, and this gathering wouldn't have been the same without the Christmas cheer Ashley had managed to sprinkle into all the dark corners of Madison's home. They'd even set up the little tabletop tree, and Ashley had drawn and cut out a stack of fleur-de-lis to place as ornaments. Callie would have loved it.

Troy finished telling an ER story that left everyone gasping then erupting into laughter, while the bluesy voice of Gary Clark, Jr. filled the room with Callie's favorite tunes. Every element of the evening was a celebration of the things and people Callie loved. A celebration of who she was. The light that was no longer with them.

Madison allowed herself to slip into the cool, dark what-if pool. The pool of imagining if Callie were still here with them—sitting on the couch beside Doug, telling her own dazzling tale of some otherwise mundane event, her head tilted back in laughter, captivating the entire room as her eyes sparkled with the Christmas lights. Bacchus would be snuggled at her feet instead of curled in his bed in the corner of the room. Her permanent reminder of *what-if.*

Her chest began to seize up, her breath quick, shallow, and painful now. Across the room, Lydia noticed the signs. She held Madison's gaze and raised her brow with a nod, willing Madison to remember the grounding exercises she'd taught her last year. Madison fought to remember. Was it five things she could feel? Or did it start with what she could see? It had been a while since she needed to do this, and the anxiety of forgetting was making this moment worse.

Letters.

She remembered the other one that worked for her.

*Z, y, x, w, v…*deep breath…*u, t, s, r, q…*

She took another deep breath, nodded to Lydia, and continued through until she felt the panic wash away.

When she finished, Madison took in the room and the people in it once again. Their smiles. Their laughter. Their warmth and light.

She was grateful Doug had convinced her to invite Lydia and Camille. A couple more people in the house felt…right. She hadn't been certain about having someone she didn't know involved in this little remembrance gathering, but it somehow took off some of the pressure. And Camille seemed nice. She was a musician. Callie would have loved her as well. Then again, Callie loved everyone, almost as much as everyone had loved Callie.

The ding of the oven saved her from another swim in a sad pool of memories. She excused herself to check on their dinner, and Doug followed her, making some excuse about needing a refill, even though he still had half of his cranberry gin fizz left in his glass.

"How you holding up?" he asked.

"I'll live," she answered. It was a one-eighty from her response to a similar question a year ago.

Madison turned off the timer and opened the oven door. The cheese was toasty and bubbly, so she pulled the casserole dish out and placed it on the stovetop. Garlic and onion and spices filled the kitchen, and Doug leaned over her shoulder to take a whiff.

"Good Jesus, I've missed this," he said.

Crawfish fettuccine had been Callie's favorite dish, and she had been the one to cook it for many of their dinner parties. She'd always been the better cook, and food had been her love language. Madison had been sure this dish died along with her, but then she found the old, stained recipe card tucked away in the back of a binder when she went through the last of Callie's things a few months ago.

Madison remembered Callie saying once that she learned to make the dish from her grandmother. Her first instinct had been to send the recipe card to some family member, but she quickly remembered that they didn't deserve any part of Callie. Not after rejecting her for coming out.

So Madison kept the card, knowing she'd one day do her best to recreate the dish they all loved almost as dearly as the woman who'd made it for them. Yesterday, when she finally realized she needed to plan the food for this event, she decided that *one day* was today.

"I hope I didn't screw it up."

Doug put his hands on her arms and kissed her cheek. "You're doing amazing. And it smells delicious. I'm proud as hell of you, darlin'."

She blinked back tears and nodded. Acknowledging the praise. Unable to speak.

Bacchus wandered into the kitchen and sat silently on the linoleum near them.

Doug wrinkled his nose. "What's wrong with him?"

"What do you mean?" Madison looked him over, but he didn't seem ill. His eyes were clear. He didn't look lethargic.

"He's just sitting there," Doug said. "He's not barking or trying to lick my face or running around trying to trip one of us into the oven, Hansel-and-Gretel-style."

Madison laughed. "That's all Ashley's doing. He's great, right?"

"The Amazing Ashley is definitely living up to her name." He shifted nervously on his heels. "We don't have to talk about that tonight though, if—"

"I'm falling for her," Madison blurted out.

"Oh." Doug stared at her, speechless for probably the first time in his life.

"Callie would want me to talk about it. So I'm talking about it." Callie hadn't been afraid of anything. Ever. And Madison couldn't think of a better way to honor Callie than to squash her own fears and admit her feelings.

"That's great. I'm happy for you. Callie would be happy for you too."

"Well, there's nothing to be happy about." She glanced down at Bacchus, still waiting patiently for a job or attention or whatever he'd wandered in there for. "I have an adopter set up for him. She's taking him after Christmas."

Doug did a poor job of trying to hide his disappointment. "It doesn't have to end that way."

"It does. I have to move on. I can't do that with him as a reminder. No matter how well-behaved he is now."

"No," he said. "I mean with you and Ashley. It doesn't have to begin *and* end with the dog."

"But it will."

"Why?"

Madison took a breath. "Because everything ends."

Doug's bright eyes faded with a sad sheen over them. It didn't look right on him, the joyous man who'd been her rock, who'd carried her through some of her darkest days with nothing more than a smile and a bit of delicious gossip to distract her. But Madison didn't have the heart to tell him everything would be okay. Didn't have the heart to lie. Not about this. Not today.

Because she knew the truth: she was destined to be alone in this world. If the universe hadn't meant to teach her that lesson, well, it wouldn't have taken so much from her.

"Maddie, darlin', I don't believe for one second that that's true." He took her face in both of his hands and made her look at him. "You *will* have a life filled with joy and happiness and someone who loves you as fiercely as I do, but you're gonna have to open your heart and take a chance again to have all of that." He gave a sad smile and let her face go. "But we'll work on that another day. Tonight, we stuff ourselves with pasta and gin."

She turned to Doug and held a gigantic serving spoon over the dish of pasta, crawfish, and cheese. "That, my dear friend, is the best idea I've heard all night."

Madison smiled and glanced back into the living room at her other three guests. This tiny circle of friends had filled her home with love and laughter and hope when she'd needed it most.

Maybe, if opening her home again turned out this well, opening her heart again might not be such a disaster either.

CHAPTER 9

Sunday morning's walk was nice and balmy compared to the previous icy morning. Although she was grateful for above freezing temperatures—even if only slightly above freezing—Ashley was less than grateful for waking up in her own bed this morning. Even though she'd only stayed in the guest room, she'd still woken to the delicious sounds and smells of Madison making pancakes in her tiny galley kitchen. Walking in on her in her pajamas with her hair tied in a loose, low bun had nearly taken Ashley's breath away. She imagined waking up to that face every morning, and her heart ached with a longing for something she never knew she wanted. Such a simple sight, and yet she imagined it was a sight she could never tire of.

Even Bacchus had a little extra spring in his step this morning with the slightly warmer temps, and Ashley had to take an occasional skip step to keep up with him. She probably should have made him heel and keep pace with her, but she wasn't in the mood to dampen anyone's enthusiasm at the moment.

They were five houses down the road when one of

Bacchus's favorite neighborhood buddies (formerly his mortal enemy) stepped out onto his own porch. The gigantic Standard Poodle, Tristan, pranced in circles while his owner, Mack, locked the door behind them.

"Good morning, guys," Ashley said.

"Good morning! Glad we're done with that ice?"

"Definitely," she replied.

Tristan trotted down the porch steps toward the sidewalk beside Mack, who was wearing his standard uniform of gray Xavier sweatpants and black and gold Xavier sweatshirt. They usually headed in a different direction for their morning walk, but their paths often crossed for a friendly greeting and butt sniffs for the dogs. Both had come a long way over the last few weeks of their interactions.

"So we're thinking about having a little thing next weekend. A party." He hesitated. "Okay, so this is totally Felicity's idea, but we're thinking about inviting all the people in the neighborhood with dogs and having a sort of Christmas party for the puppers. You're invited too, of course. And Bacchus's owner. Uh…"

"Madison." She wasn't judging. No one in the neighborhood knew Madison's name since she never went anywhere but straight to her car. But if she managed to stick around, maybe she could convince Madison to walk with them some times when the weather turned nice. Maybe she could lure her out with blooming azaleas.

But that would be three months from now. Ashley wasn't even sure what the situation might be three weeks from now, much less three months. But her planning drive couldn't help think at least a little about *what if*.

"Right, right. So you and Madison and Bacchus should all come over next Saturday."

"That sounds like fun," Ashley said. "I'd love to come, and I'll let Madison know."

"Great. Well, let me get this beast moving." He waved and headed off in the opposite direction. "Y'all have a good walk."

"You too!"

Ashley pulled Bacchus along until he gave up on following his giant furry friend and continued walking beside her instead. It was a far cry from the disastrous pulling and lunging and barking that made up their initial encounters just a couple short weeks ago. He was practically a different dog now. Amazing what a little consistency and a whole lot of patience and determination could do.

And if patience and determination could make that drastic a turnaround in just two weeks, what could happen for Bacchus and Madison down the road?

Of all the things Ashley could have expected to run across this morning, a puppy party was nowhere near that list. But it sounded like a blast! And if she could convince Madison to come along, and if Bacchus could show her how much fun they could have together hanging out with a bunch of neighbors…

Ashley had been struggling to think of a way to keep those two together, but Mack might have just dropped the key to success right in her lap.

Madison stared in awe at her newly redesigned photography site as the afternoon sunlight streamed in through her window. A carousel of some of her best work scrolled at the top of the crisp, clean homepage featuring her brand new logo. It was absolutely gorgeous.

She clicked through her portfolio and contact pages as a

key rattled in the front door. A moment later, she heard Ashley greeting Bacchus in the living room. Besides being incredibly good at her job with Bacchus, Ashley had proven herself completely trustworthy. Giving her a key to the apartment earlier that week— so she could walk Bacchus any time without them having to coordinate schedules—had been an easy decision.

Maybe too easy.

After she'd confessed her feelings to Doug, and after she'd cried herself to sleep last night holding tight to her memories, Madison had spent most of her Sunday morning thinking about where she was at this moment in her life. And what she wanted from this moment on.

Over the last few weeks, Ashley had somehow become an integral part of her daily life. It had happened gradually, but it was becoming harder and harder for Madison to imagine her life without Ashley. As good as leaning on Ashley felt, Madison couldn't let herself depend on another person again. Not when she was just starting to put her life back together.

Rebuilding her foundation had to come first now. No matter how much she was growing to love whatever was building between them, she couldn't get derailed by a relationship right now. She couldn't afford a setback. Especially not this time of year.

So maybe it really was time for Ashley to go. Even if the thought tied Madison's stomach in knots and made her want to lose her mind and call Bacchus's adopter to cancel the whole thing. She knew this was for the best. For everyone.

But Bacchus didn't have to leave for another few weeks, which meant Ashley didn't have to leave just yet either.

"Hey, give me a sec, I'll walk with you guys." She could

totally keep things professional and still enjoy their company for the time being.

"Oh," Ashley said, attaching the leash to Bacchus's collar. "I was trying not to disturb you if you were working."

Madison saved her work quickly and hurried to meet them by the door where she rushed to lace up her shoes. "I've been working for a while. I could use the break."

"We were going for a pretty long walk. Bacchus seems to do better in the evenings when he gets out a lot of his energy in the afternoon."

"Honestly? I probably would do better if I got some exercise in the afternoon too." She tied her laces, then hopped to her feet.

Ashley laughed. "We probably all would. Are you sure?"

Madison didn't seem to be sure of anything lately. But she had finally decided to move forward anyway. To make decisions. To get out of the house and to live her life. And it felt good. She wanted to keep that feeling and momentum rolling.

And, truthfully, she kind of liked hanging out with Bacchus now. He really was a sweet pup, and now that his bad habits were in check, she had fewer reasons to keep him at a distance. What could she say? The dude was growing on her.

"I'm sure. Besides, you've done such a great job with him, I kind of like hanging out with this beast now." She scratched his ear then froze. "If you're okay with me tagging along?"

"Of course!" Ashley beamed with glee, her sleek black hair hanging over the shoulders of her bright red puffy coat. "He's your dog. And he does like to show off for you."

Madison couldn't help wonder if that was the only reason Ashley was excited about Madison tagging along. She couldn't stop herself from thinking that maybe Ashley was as excited to have Madison's company as Madison was to spend a nice long walk chatting with Ashley.

Madison shook those thoughts from her head. *Exercise.* She was doing this for exercise and fresh air and to get a jump start on her day. Not to flirt with her employee. Not to chat and giggle and connect with a woman who would soon be out of her life anyway.

Who was she kidding? She was utterly hopeless.

Madison grabbed her coat and noticed the wide smile and the sparkle in Ashley's eyes, and her heart fluttered realizing she wasn't the only one swimming in the deep end.

CHAPTER 10

By the time they turned the corner putting Madison's duplex in view at the end of the block, Bacchus was fully worn out and ready to go home. Mission accomplished.

Except now Ashley was the one who wasn't ready to finish their walk.

She'd been shocked when Madison had decided to join them. After all, part of the whole point of Ashley hanging around was to give Madison time away from Bacchus. Madison's eager smile and bounce in her step as she followed them out were quite unexpected.

Not that Ashley was complaining.

She walked down the sidewalk with Bacchus loose-leash on one side and Madison on her other side, hands stuffed in the pockets of her comfy brown barn coat. Her plan to help Bacchus win over Madison and convince her to keep him was off to a fantastic start. But while Bacchus was being the perfect canine gentleman, following her lead and never pulling once, Ashley felt the urge to be much less well-behaved.

She wanted nothing more than to slip her arm around

Madison's and lean against her as they walked together. Madison's perfume—fresh and floral with a hint of citrus—grew stronger as they walked, her body heat intensifying the enticingly flirty scent. It was downright intoxicating.

Her companion's scent mingled with the magical sounds of holiday jazz renditions floating out from shops and a crisp December chill nipping at their exposed cheeks. So far, this holiday season had been everything Ashley could ever want…only now all she wanted was Madison.

It was wrong. Madison was her employer. You don't make out with the boss. Much less any of the other things Ashley wanted to do with Madison. But Ashley had given up denying to herself that this was exactly what she wanted… and more.

Ever since Friday night, Ashley couldn't stop thinking about how it felt to stand side by side with her in that kitchen. How doing something as mundane as cooking pasta together had felt more magical than anything Ashley had ever felt before. She had nothing to compare to how much she felt drawn to this woman. She'd never felt this strongly for anyone before. And the more she tried to make Madison fall for Bacchus, the deeper Ashley fell.

They didn't talk much, mostly pointed out cute holiday decorations in the neighborhood as they inhaled the crisp December air and admired the gorgeous sky palette the setting sun had created for them. Ashley searched desperately for some excuse to continue their walk, but Bacchus began pulling the second he reached the property line and dragged her up the front steps to the porch.

"Hey, have you been to Luna Fête this year?" Madison's voice was thin and light, lacking its usual heaviness. An edge of hope lining each word.

"No." In truth, Ashley had never been to the annual

Central Business District event. She always meant to, but she just never made it out there.

"Do you want to? It's the last night," Madison said. "We could check it out, then maybe grab a bite and drinks somewhere nearby. My treat. I owe you for that fabulous work on my website and logo."

"Oh, please," she said. "I was glad to do that. And that was thanks for letting me crash here Friday night. We're even."

Madison grinned. "Not by a mile. I love the work you did. If you ever decide to start a business doing that, please let me write your first glowing testimonial."

Ashley felt her cheeks blush warm with the praise. She'd never even considered starting her own freelance thing after the layoff. Sure, she could do the work, but running her own business? With spreadsheets and budgets and trackers…all of that sounded way beyond her capabilities.

They went inside, got Bacchus settled, used the restroom, then Madison locked up behind them. A moment later, they were in Madison's car heading toward the Central Business District.

Parking was a bit of a nightmare, even considering it was a Sunday evening. It seemed everyone had the same idea to bring their whole families out to Lafayette Square for the last night of this little festival.

They approached the crowds taking over the block, and Ashley was stunned by the display of lights. Colorful illuminated sculptures dotted the landscape and gorgeous animated light projections blanketed many of the buildings. The front of Gallier Hall was currently displaying colorful images of snowballs between candy-striped columns. Children hopped nearby over interactive circles of light as if they were lily pads. It was an absolute technological wonderland.

"Pretty, right?" Madison's face glowed with amusement.

Such a refreshing change from the woman Ashley had met just a few short weeks ago.

They wandered around the area, strolling slowly down the sidewalks and following the flow of the crowds through the CBD while children giggled and crisscrossed their path.

Ashley wanted to reach out and take Madison's hand as they walked. Felt the urge deep in her bones.

Instead, she inched closer and closer, until their jacket sleeves touched, occasionally pressing shoulders and arms together when they stopped to marvel at a display or listen to a brass band passing by. That simple act filled Ashley with so much joy, she wanted to turn and take Madison's face in her hands and kiss her in the middle of the Square.

But like Bacchus had learned to control his urges, so had Ashley.

When they circled back to where they'd started, Madison suggested they grab a bite at a restaurant a couple blocks away. She said it was a favorite spot of hers and wanted to treat Ashley, and she wasn't taking no for an answer. Ashley was on such a high that she would have agreed to anything at that moment.

A few minutes later, they were inside a cute little restaurant/bar with a hippie vibe, sitting at a small cafe table with scrolled ironwork. The server suggested the weekend drink special, the Holiday Smash, which they both ordered along with brie and fig jam grilled cheeses. When the drinks arrived, Ashley took a sip, and the deep, rich bourbon and bright, fresh satsuma and cranberry immediately warmed her insides.

"Oh that is delicious," she said.

Madison moaned into her glass and nodded in agreement.

"So how has the rest of your weekend been?" Ashley asked.

It felt odd to make small talk with Madison, but she wasn't sure what else to say. They were in this weird relational limbo where they saw each other nearly every day but didn't know a whole lot about each other.

Coworkers.

She'd just described coworkers in her head. Because that's what they were.

It was easy to forget that sometimes, but Madison was her boss, and they saw each other because Ashley had a job to do. She needed to remember that, to focus on that, especially since she had a mission that involved keeping this job.

But these weren't exactly office hours at the moment.

"I had a few friends over last night, for drinks and dinner," Madison said.

"That sounds nice. Like an early Christmas party or something?"

Madison paused. "It was the anniversary of Callie's death."

"Oh, I'm so sorry." Then she put the timeline together, realizing she'd been there for the first part of that day, crashing Madison's mourning and memories. "Crap, I'm sorry, I—"

"No, no, no." Madison waved her hands in front of her. "Nothing to apologize for. It was good to have some company. And the party was nice. Just four friends over for drinks and dinner. It was…a celebration. Just like Callie would have wanted."

"Well, that does sound nice. I'm glad you had people to be with you for that."

"It was." Madison gave a small, hesitant smile. "We used to have these big dinner parties all the time, and then…well, I haven't had anyone over like that in quite a while. But it made me think it might be nice to start doing that again."

Ashley could see from the strain and longing in Madison's face that this was more than just dinner and drinks and company. This was about Madison realizing it might be nice to *live* again. And seeing that realization made Ashley happier than it ought to, happier than she had a right to feel.

"That sounds like a really good idea."

"I'm thinking of maybe doing something for Christmas Eve. If I can pull it together, I'd love for you to be there." Her hesitation transformed into a clumsy, headlong rush over her words. "I mean, I'm sure you have plans, but you're welcome to come, even if it's just for a minute or two."

A wide smile took over Ashley's face, despite her intention to play it cool here. *This is your boss*, she tried to remind herself. *This is basically an office party, be cool.* But there was no stopping her joy. "Yes, of course. I'd love to."

Madison took another sip of her drink. "Great. Hopefully, I get everything worked out to pull this off."

"Let me know if I can help you with anything," Ashley said. Then, she seized her opening. "And speaking of parties."

A brief hint of terror flashed across Madison's face, but she quickly masked it and tilted her head in interest.

"When I was out walking Bacchus this morning, I ran into one of your neighbors. They're having a thing next Saturday, and they wanted to invite you."

"Oh." Madison's nose did an adorable little scrunchy thing. "I don't really know any of my neighbors. There are a lot of new people, and I haven't exactly been…social this last year."

"That's okay because they know Bacchus. Or at least they do now. We've run into them a bunch during our morning walks. It's the couple with the big, black Standard Poodle."

Recognition hit. "Ah, right. I don't think I even know their names."

"Felicity and Mack," said Ashley. "Their dog is Tristan."

"They seem nice, but I don't really think I know them well enough to show up at a party."

"You don't, but Bacchus does."

Madison laughed. "I don't think they want Bacchus crashing their holiday party."

"Actually, that's exactly what they want." Ashley smiled, too dang full of herself as she delivered the news. "It's a dog party. They're inviting all their friends and neighbors with puppies and dogs to bring them over for a dog-Christmas-themed shindig."

"You can't be serious."

"I would never joke about a puppy party. Doesn't it sound like a dream come true?" She was trying to will her own enthusiasm to infect Madison and convince her to say yes.

Her whole plan for the rest of the month hinged on Madison going to this party with her and Bacchus. They would go to this thing together and Bacchus would win everyone over with his newfound charm and pizzazz, and Madison would have such a good time and be so smitten with him that she would cancel the whole adoption plan. Then she and Bacchus could stay together and Ashley could stay in their orbit too.

All she needed was one yes from Madison, and all the dominoes would fall into place.

"I don't know. I mean, if you want to take him, that would be great. I'm sure you'd both have fun."

"*You* could have fun too. You're allowed some fun now and then."

Madison hesitated, but she said, "I'll think about it. It

might be fun." She looked around. "I'm going to run to the restroom before our food gets here."

Ashley watched her disappear down a dark hallway, the buzz from the strong drink she'd sipped far too quickly dared her to follow the gorgeous brunette.

No. If Bacchus could control himself, so could she.

Except Bacchus had never been introduced to a Holiday Smash during one of their testing sessions.

A buzzing from behind Madison's drink glass caught her attention, and she saw that Madison had left her phone. It rang more, vibrating quietly on the table. Ashley couldn't help but notice the woman's name flashing on the screen with {Bacchus} behind it.

Ashley knew she should let the phone ring. Let it go to voicemail. Let Madison deal with it when she came back.

But her chest tightened, and with every buzzing ring, her hand inched closer until it wrapped around the purple phone case.

"Hello?"

"Hello, this is Linda, we spoke about me taking Bacchus after Christmas."

"Yes." Ashley forced herself to breathe. There was no reason to panic. This woman was probably calling to say she couldn't take him after all. She changed her mind or her circumstances changed.

"Well, I was calling to say that my travel plans were canceled, so I could take him as soon as next weekend if that works out for you."

The vice grip around Ashley's heart cranked tighter. Next weekend. That wasn't enough time to convince Madison to keep him. Sure Madison was warming up to him, but Ashley needed more than a week to really sell this. She needed those three weeks.

In a panic, she said, "I'm sorry, I can't. In fact, I'm not sure I can part with him after all."

"Oh." The woman's eager tone dropped with the weight of disappointment. "I thought…"

"I'm really sorry," Ashley said.

And she was. She was so sorry she was lying to this woman. That she was making decisions like this behind Madison's back. That she couldn't let this person have Bacchus. Not now. Not when she was so close to making everything right.

"Well, if you change your mind or just need some more time, you have my number."

"I do. Thank you."

Ashley ended the call and returned the phone to the table just before Madison rounded the corner. Her smile lit up the dark table more than the tea light candle. She was glowing. Relaxed. Happy, for the first time since Ashley had met her. Bacchus had been a part of that, part of getting Madison out of the house and living her life again.

So why did Ashley feel so guilty?

She knew why. Because she'd betrayed Madison's trust. Because she'd overridden Madison's plans. Because if Ashley's plan didn't work out, she might have just ruined Bacchus's best shot at a happy life with someone who really wanted him.

But that wasn't true. Madison loved him. She just didn't think she could keep him. But she would realize that. Soon. Ashley would make sure of it.

And if she didn't?

She loved Bacchus. If she couldn't convince Madison to keep him, and Madison couldn't find another home, Ashley would take him in. She'd find another apartment if she had to. She would make this right. One way or another.

❋

MADISON STUMBLED as she hit the bottom step out of the little cafe where she and Ashley had just spent the last hour chatting and drinking and giggling.

Giggling.

She'd blame the bourbon, but she'd only had two drinks. Besides, alcohol wasn't the problem. Being around Ashley made Madison lightheaded, like she could float away hand in hand with this woman. Nothing felt heavy or dark anymore. Spending an evening with Ashley was the equivalent of the displays they'd just explored: a gorgeous showcase of light in the face of darkness.

She felt silly and childish and a flood of other emotions, but she didn't care. She didn't worry about anything with Ashley by her side.

"Do you want to take another walk around the block," Ashley asked, rubbing her hands together to warm them before stuffing them in her coat pockets. "Walk off those drinks before we drive back?"

"Yeah, sure." Madison edged closer as they walked, so their coat sleeves were touching each other. It was the most intimacy Madison had had in over a year. And she wanted more. So much more. But she was sober enough to control her urges, most notably the urge to slip her arm around Ashley's and rest her head on Ashley's shoulder as they walked.

Lafayette Square was still filled with people checking out the lights, and she wasn't quite in the mood to enter the crowd again. In a weird way she didn't quite understand, Madison didn't want to share this tiny moment with anyone other than Ashley. So she pointed at an unoccupied metal bench at the edge of the square near an illuminated sign that read: *Magic is something you make.*

"How about we sit here for a minute?"

"Sure," Ashley said as they both sat on the bench.

Madison realized this evening had been the first time she and Ashley had been alone together. Like…really alone. Without Bacchus. As much as she'd been growing more and more fond of the guy, she was growing even more fond of having Ashley all to herself.

She shouldn't.

Most definitely not.

But…she was. She really, really was.

"So," she said, stalling while her brain struggled to find something new to talk about. Something that wasn't Bacchus or Callie. They'd already talked about their favorite TV shows. Already bonded over their shared love of *Brooklyn 99* and agreed that Madison was definitely an Amy and Ashley was definitely a Jake. And then the conversation screeched to a halt and Madison had excused herself to go to the restroom. Again.

Now she didn't know what else to bring up since she was the absolute worst at small talk. She didn't really go to the movies or to see local bands or any of the other things she could think of.

Then Ashley saved them both by asking, "Do you have any shoots booked this week?"

That Madison could talk about. "A bridal shoot midweek. Hopefully, the weather holds out. And then I'm shooting some big local company's Christmas party on Friday night."

"Ooh, any company I know?" Excitement and hunger for gossip dripped from her voice. It was downright cute.

Madison laughed. "Advertising firm."

"Have you ever done a gallery show?" Ashley asked. "Like

of your street photography? Because those photos in your living room are fantastic."

Madison felt her cheeks blush. "Thanks. I had been thinking about it a while back. One of Callie's friends knew someone who owned a gallery, and we were talking about maybe setting something up last spring." She sighed. "But then stuff happened."

"I'm sorry."

"No, don't be. It just wasn't meant to be then. I haven't really even thought about it since. It was sort of Callie's thing she wanted me to do."

"You didn't want to do the show?"

"No, I did. I guess." She paused and thought about how to explain how she felt about the whole thing. "I just…I just don't really allow myself big dreams. It's not that I don't think I can do it, it's more that I don't like to be disappointed if it doesn't work out. I'd rather make peace and be comfortable with life the way it is, and if anything exciting happens then it's a happy surprise."

Ashley tilted her head like a confused puppy. "That makes sense. I guess."

"Not the way you operate, I take it?"

"Not exactly."

Madison fought back a smile. It wasn't at all the way she'd seen Ashley operate. She'd shown up for her job interview overflowing with confidence and big dreams and absolutely no experience to back those up. It was one of the things Madison admired most about her. Her big dreams and her boundless optimism.

"So if you *were* going to allow yourself some big dreams, what would they be?"

Madison raised her eyebrows. "That's a sneaky question."

"And the answer is?"

There was that bluster and relentless determination of hers. Gosh, she loved this woman.

Wait. No.

Madison focused on the question at hand, a welcome alternative to the intruding thoughts she absolutely did not want to analyze. "I don't know. Maybe a gallery show would be nice. More regular bookings…like I'd love to be booked up so much I need to have a cancellation list. Oh, and health insurance would be nice."

Ashley laughed out loud at that. "I love that your big dream is health insurance."

"What? It is big! That's expensive."

"No kidding. But it's pretty adorable that it's at the top of your big dreams list." Her face froze as she looked down at her hand, which she'd placed on Madison's leg when she'd let out that last laugh. It had been such a natural move that neither of them had noticed, except now she wasn't taking that hand away.

Madison realized with a sudden and overwhelming certainty that she absolutely did not want her to take that hand away.

When Ashley looked back up, her hand still on Madison's leg, she stared into Madison's eyes. Madison stared back. She didn't want to stop staring, but she felt her body moving closer and her eyes closing and…

What was she doing?

But her brain was still a little fuzzy, so instead of talking herself out of this, her hand went up to Ashley's face as she met Ashley's mouth with her own. Her lips were soft and the chill in them warmed quickly. Madison placed soft kisses on Ashley's mouth, and after the brief initial shock of contact wore off, Ashley relaxed against her and returned those kisses with her own, tasting of that sweet, smoky bourbon mixed with tart orange and cranberry from their drinks.

Ashley squeezed Madison's thigh with that hand that she never bothered to remove, sending heat waves all the way up Madison's leg. Her soft kisses intensified, desire rolling through her now in huge crashing waves.

Big dreams.

Madison hadn't allowed herself to fully realize that this was one of them.

She froze, then pulled her head back, leaving her hand on the side of Ashley's confused face. Searching to make sense of it all, to make sense of what she'd done, Madison could only say, "I'm sorry."

Ashley put her own hand on Madison's and said, "No, it's fine."

"But it isn't." Big dreams or not, she was still Ashley's *boss*. This was extremely inappropriate. Worse than inappropriate. "I shouldn't have. I'm sorry."

Ashley removed both of her hands and scooted on the bench, her eyes swirling with confusion and sadness and hurt. "It's fine. I understand."

Madison wanted to grab her again. To hold her close and make her understand that it wasn't her. It wasn't even ghosts coming between them. This was Madison shutting things down that shouldn't be. She had known better than to act on her urges, but she'd gotten caught up in the evening and their conversation and Ashley's delightful presence. She was still Bacchus's owner and Ashley's boss for the next three weeks.

Kisses in the park weren't a thing she was allowed to have. Not with this woman. Not with anyone she cared about, apparently.

"We should probably go," she said.

Ashley nodded in agreement, so they stood from the bench and walked to Madison's car together in silence.

CHAPTER 11

ASHLEY SLIPPED A SPARKLY GREEN TANK TOP OVER HER HEAD. After she pulled her arms through it, she stood in front of her bedroom mirror and smoothed the fabric. It was much warmer than it had been a week ago but still December and still chilly in the evening, so she grabbed her favorite slim black blazer from the closet.

"So is that standard puppy party attire?" Theresa asked as she leaned against the door frame in her December uniform of festive fleece pants and oversized sweatshirt.

Ashley shrugged. "I have no idea." She was imagining tacky sweaters or sweatshirts with dogs' faces airbrushed on them. But no way in this universe would she show up like that. At any kind of party. And if she got paw prints on her jacket, well, that's what dry cleaners were for. Thankfully she still had a job to pay for that.

"I'm assuming Madison is going with you?"

"Yes." She tried to keep her voice steady, but her tone still had a slight wobble to it. Everything wobbled whenever she talked about Madison, thought about Madison, or even stood in Madison's presence.

Madison. Her boss.

The woman she *kissed* last weekend.

Ashley shook that memory from her mind and grabbed her bag. No point dwelling on that. Madison made it perfectly clear that wouldn't be happening again.

"Are you gonna finally make a move of your own, or are you planning to keep pretending like there's nothing going on with you two?" Apparently, Theresa had no plans to let this go.

"There are no moves to be made. She isn't ready," Ashley said. "Plus, the whole she's still my boss thing."

Theresa waved a dismissive hand. "Details."

Details Ashley couldn't exactly gloss over. Especially when Madison almost completely shut down after that kiss last Sunday night. They'd driven back to Madison's house in silence, only to have her apologize once again before going inside. Ashley didn't see her again until Wednesday evening. She was always hiding out somewhere or working at the computer with her back to the door when Ashley came over to walk Bacchus. But when Ashley had arrived for his Wednesday evening walk, Madison was waiting in the living room with a polite smile and another apology. This time the apology had been for being reclusive.

Ever since then, things had gone back to normal, running into each other and making small talk, but the vibe between them was stiff and awkward. Ashley was actually surprised Madison still decided to tag along for the party that evening.

Surprised, but glad.

She still had work to do. She still wanted to help Bacchus and Madison stay together. And while Madison might not be ready for kissing in the park right now, Ashley hoped to stick around for whenever she did feel ready. Because she was more than ready for more kissing.

That kiss with Madison had made her dizzy with want and hungry for more. But she was willing to wait as long as Madison needed.

She waved her keys in the air and winked at Theresa. "Don't wait up."

"Oh, don't worry," Theresa called out as Ashley headed for the door. "I'll definitely be waiting to hear all about this!"

MADISON STARED in wonder out the passenger window of Ashley's car. With only a week and a half until Christmas, almost every house down this stretch of St. Charles was lit up for the holidays. The trees along the road were lit up as well, making a sort of on-ramp into holiday-land.

This old neighborhood was always gorgeous—old money gorgeous—but it was especially so this time of year. Even during the day time, green garland and red and gold ribbons adorned front porches and porch swings and enormous wreaths welcomed onlookers.

"So why did we have to drive out here?" Madison asked. Ashley had shown up a little while ago, a big smile on her face and keys in hand on Madison's porch. "I thought you said this party was for one of my neighbors?"

"Apparently he invited too many people." Ashley tilted her head toward Madison in the passenger seat. "Your neighborhood has a *lot* of dogs it seems. So he moved the party to his mom's house. Or his in-law's. Someone fancier, I don't know."

"Fancier? We're taking a neighborhood full of dogs someplace fancy?"

Ashley just shrugged while she kept her eyes on the road and dug in her pocket. She handed Madison a scrap of paper with an address scribbled on it. "Here, navigate for me."

Madison shook her head, more amused than annoyed. They were halfway down St. Charles, but Ashley just now thought to get detailed directions. Her breezy confidence in the face of having no idea where they were going was an enviable trait, and downright adorable.

Madison took the paper and pulled out her phone, but she didn't need to. She recognized the address immediately. It was the same road where Callie used to visit a gallery owned by an elderly artist couple. "Oh, that's just up ahead. A couple blocks on the right, I think."

A few seconds later, Ashley made a right turn onto a road packed with cars on both sides. Madison took a deep breath and hoped this was just a sign that everyone was home on a Saturday night, and that these weren't all their fellow party guests.

Ashley slipped into an empty spot near the end of the block, and the three of them walked toward the house with a "Winter Wufferland" banner hanging from the porch entrance. Bacchus walked with Ashley, loose-leash but anxiously taking in all the smells of this new neighborhood. He was handling it all surprisingly well.

When they climbed the porch steps, Ashley knocked on the front door. With all the noise coming from inside, Madison was convinced this would prove to be a colossal mistake. Then Ashley slipped her hand in Madison's and gave it a reassuring squeeze, and suddenly everything felt right. Madison felt like she could tackle anything, everything, even a *dog* party, with Ashley by her side.

But when the door opened and they stepped inside, the scene took Madison's breath away and replaced it with a steep anxiety spiral.

"Um, what is happening here?" A rat terrier skipped over her navy canvas flats. "There are dogs *everywhere*."

Literally *everywhere*.

Two Yorkies sat on a beige couch while a gigantic black Lab slept in a ball on the floor. A pair of unrelated mutts dashed down the hall with reindeer antlers strapped to their heads. A particularly prissy Maltese was even sitting on the bar while a woman fed him Santa-shaped biscuits.

Ashley laughed as she tried to contain Bacchus lunging to follow the reindeer mutts. "What did you think when I said it was a puppy party?"

"I don't know," Madison said, catching a whiff of gingerbread mixed with wet mutt. "That it was a puppy-themed people party? Maybe the dogs would play in the backyard or something?" She surveyed the chaotic scene again and fought the urge to bail. Ashley and Bacchus could have plenty of fun without her. "This is…a lot."

Ashley looked sympathetic, but there was a tiny twinkle in her eye that made Madison question if there had been a wee bit of mischievous deception at play here. "Sorry, I should have explained better."

"No, I was in denial, I guess." She fell into an easy smile. Everything around Ashley had been so easy, right from the start.

And then she'd ruined everything with that kiss.

Ever since that night last weekend, Madison couldn't stop thinking about her. How she wanted to stroll through the streets every evening with her. How she wanted to reach out and hold her hand. How she'd wanted to invite her inside again once they returned to Madison's duplex…and not to sleep in the guest room this time.

She'd realized that she was looking forward to Ashley's visits more and more every day, and not just because the woman got Bacchus out of her hair for a little while. She looked forward to those visits because they meant time with Ashley. Time that turned into awkward silence after she'd made her move without thinking things through first. Without a proper conversation about how to handle things between them.

The anxiety she felt now with all of these dogs running around and Bacchus eager to cut loose with them…that anxiety was just a mirror for what was already swirling inside of her. The anxiety leading up to the conversation she wanted to have with Ashley before this night was over.

"Oh, here." Ashley held out the end of Bacchus's leash and pointed to the far side of the living room. "I'm gonna say hi and let Greg know we're here, but I'm *not* taking Bacchus through that gauntlet of terriers until he gets settled a little in here first."

She looked down at Bacchus, his long happy face smiling up at her. Then she looked back at Ashley. "Okay. Sure. We'll…wait here. I guess."

Ashley smiled as she placed a hand on Madison's arm. Even through her leather jacket, Madison could feel the heat of that touch. She wanted to grab hold of Ashley and beg *don't leave.*

But that was a conversation for later.

Ashley slipped away into the crowd, weaving around furniture and dogs and owners with a confident, exuberant grace and charm that Madison had grown to love more than she ever could have imagined. She stood there, alone, holding Bacchus's leash. To her surprise, she was quite comfortable being solely responsible for him in a public place, even *this* place.

Even though she hadn't heard back from the woman who was supposed to adopt him in two weeks, the plan hadn't changed. And with his excellent behavior these days, it wouldn't be hard at all to find someone else to take him. Because as much as she'd grown to like the dog, she still knew he would be better off with someone else, someone who would be a better fit for him.

She smiled across the room at Ashley, who tucked a long strand of black hair behind her ears and cheerfully greeted a bearded man and the huge Poodle at his feet. Ashley looked gorgeous in a black blazer over a shiny green tank and tight dark wash jeans.

Madison was beginning to realize that while she and Bacchus might not be a great fit, Ashley might very well be her perfect fit.

No matter how much she'd tried to deny it or how much she fought it, she couldn't help falling for this woman, the one who brought out the best in her. The one who made her smile and feel alive again. Tonight, she would tell her all of that. Tonight, she would tell Ashley that she wanted to continue seeing her, outside of their business arrangement, even after Bacchus was out of the picture.

Her phone dinged in her inside jacket pocket, so Madison gripped Bacchus's leash tightly and dug the phone out with her other free hand. She'd apparently forgotten to mute her email notifications for the weekend. Distracted by the promise of puppies, she supposed. But when she looked at the sender, she was unexpectedly pleased by her forgetfulness. It was the woman who'd wanted to adopt Bacchus, the one she'd been waiting to hear from.

Madison opened the email, her cheeks quite flushed and sore from all the smiling already that evening. This would be the icing on the puppy party cake. All of her plans were falling into place, and she couldn't wait to have her conversation with Ashley after this party.

As she read the email, however, her smile fell and her mood deflated rapidly, leaving her filled with disbelief and a gaping hole in her heart. The heart she should have known better than to follow.

ASHLEY MADE her way back through the living room toward Bacchus and Madison near the kitchen. Madison looked so comfortable hanging with the dog in her baggy, off-shoulder black sweater and her hair tied in a loose ponytail.

She was so glad she'd been able to convince Madison to come to this, even though she knew it wasn't exactly her thing. Selfishly she just wanted to hang out more with Madison, but another night out with people seemed like such a good thing for her too. She'd get to meet some new friends, hang out with her neighbors, breathe more fun into her life again.

Bit by bit it seemed like Madison was coming out of her reclusive grief shell. She seemed lighter. Happier. More… Madison. Her plan was working.

By the time Ashley reached her, Madison was still staring down at her phone, not at all looking so light or happy anymore.

"What's wrong?" she asked.

Madison looked up from the phone, her jaw slack and her eyes brimming with pain. It was as if the last few weeks never happened and Madison was lost all over again.

"Madison? What happened?"

She firmed up her jaw as she stared at Ashley in disbelief. "Did you talk to Bacchus's adopter?"

"I…what?" Ashley's stomach sank as she scrambled to make sense of what was happening. To process her plans crumbling before her. She looked down at the phone in Madison's hand and forced her voice into a perky pitch. "Did you hear back from her?"

"Email." The word came out low and clipped. Madison held Ashley in her gaze. "She wanted me to know that she was still interested *if I changed my mind again*. Only, I never changed my mind in the first place." She swallowed and blinked in silence several times. Then, she asked, "Did you call her?"

"I...I don't even have her number."

Ashley's heart hammered against her chest.

No, no, no.

She was so close. Things were going so well. It couldn't all fall apart like this now.

Madison's eyes softened as she pleaded, "Please don't play games with me."

Her plea broke Ashley. "She called. Last weekend, while you went to the restroom."

"What. Did. You. Do?"

"I...you needed more time." Her voice trembled along with the rest of her. "I answered the call. She thought I was you, so I didn't correct her."

"I needed more time?" Madison's brow wrinkled in confusion. Then, a bark down the hall caught their attention, and as Bacchus pulled against the leash, Madison's eyes widened. "Is that what coming here was all about? Was this some big plan to manipulate me? To convince me somehow of what *you* think is best for me?"

Her voice raised in pitch and decibel with every word, until the conversations around them evaporated and all that was left were the sounds of puppy wrestling and Mariah Carey belting out what she wants for Christmas. Madison's words stung, but they were dead on target, and Ashley couldn't deny them. Except for one tiny detail.

"I wasn't trying to manipulate you."

"Well, what would you call it?"

"I…I just hoped you'd fall in love with Bacchus." *And me.* But judging by the disgust and rage evident on Madison's face, there was no chance of that now. If there had ever been a chance.

"That isn't up to you."

"I know."

"You lied to her. And you didn't tell me about the call at all. About lying to her."

"I know." She glanced around as eyes watched them from every corner. Ashley hated being the center of attention. She hated that they could all see her flushed cheeks and the tears forming in her eyes. Hated that she had an audience as she tried to talk her way out of this. When she knew there was no defense.

Except one.

"If you really didn't want to keep him I was going to—"

"I don't care." Madison's words were icy and final.

She wanted to bare her heart. She wanted to tell Madison that this was about more than just Bacchus, that when her phone had flashed with that number and Bacchus's name she'd panicked at the thought of losing her connection to Madison. But judging by the tone of Madison's voice, she didn't think it would matter.

And why would it? She'd still lied. Betrayed Madison's trust. It didn't matter why.

She'd been so afraid of losing Madison, she'd done the one thing guaranteed to push her away.

Ashley looked around at the festivities still carrying on despite their argument, which felt more like a breakup, even though they weren't really together. "I can take you home if you don't want to stay." She held out her hand for the leash but avoided eye contact. She couldn't stand the disappointment there.

"No. He's my dog. I'll take him for a walk and call for a ride." She waited a beat, then added, "Don't worry, I'll pay you for the full night."

More than anything else, those words seared through Ashley's heart like a hot dagger. Because they reinforced what she'd feared all along. What her delusions had let her forget. Madison was her boss. Nothing more.

Ashley nodded slightly and looked down at Bacchus. She wanted to squat and hold his scruffy face and kiss his nose before she left. To tell him goodbye, probably forever.

But Madison was right. He wasn't her dog.

She turned and headed for the front door. She'd never even had a chance to take off her jacket.

Madison and Bacchus walked down the steps behind her, then split off in the opposite direction once they hit the sidewalk. Ashley turned to watch them walk away, and Bacchus turned a few times to see why she wasn't following them.

She wanted to call after them. To beg Madison to stop and hear her out. To give Ashley another chance.

But she knew she didn't deserve it. No matter how much it broke her heart to watch them leave.

Finally, she headed down the road to her car, alone. When she pulled the keys from her pocket, the bag of training treats fell out.

She sat on the curb beside them, her head in her hands, and began to sob, certain the tears would never stop. Certain she'd lost the one real bit of true holiday magic she'd ever known.

CHAPTER 12

THE ROUSES MARKET ON BARONNE WAS MORE CROWDED THAN Madison had ever seen it, especially for a Monday afternoon. Everyone in the Warehouse District and beyond was out getting supplies for Christmas Eve dinners and parties the next day. Thankfully, she had Doug with her to navigate the crowds and tackle her shopping list. Not that he had a choice. She'd only agreed to host this Christmas Eve dinner party under the condition that he help with the planning and prep.

They'd started with the dry goods first, then the seafood counter, then the liquor section, and now they were finishing up in the produce and deli area. She reached for a container of blue cheese in the refrigerated display case.

"Is that for the salad?" Doug asked.

She looked down at the plastic tub, questioning her choice. It seemed she was questioning all her life choices lately, so why not this one as well. "No, to go on the salmon."

He placed a hand to his chest and recoiled in horror. "I'm sorry, have you lost your mind?"

"There was a recipe. In a Pinterest email." She left out the part about how it made her stomach turn, but the thought of looking up recipes sounded even more torturous, so she went with the email one.

"No. Absolutely not." He grabbed the blue cheese from her hand and placed it back in the case. "I don't care what recipe you saw, I will not allow you to serve blue cheese on good fish." Doug gave her a long, sympathetic stare and sighed heavily. "Listen, you know I love you. And I fully support a good mope. But I cannot condone crimes against salmon."

"I'm not moping."

"Sure you aren't."

She was pretty sure she wasn't. She'd done the right thing after all. Ashley had betrayed her, so whatever had been building between them had to end before it started. There was nothing to mope about.

Although the three empty pints of Blue Bell Christmas Cookies flavored ice cream in her trash can would probably argue differently.

"Will that dapper, hairy beast still be around for tomorrow evening's festivities? I want to at least say goodbye before he goes. When is that woman taking him?"

Madison moved the cart over to grab a bag of fresh cranberries and toss them in her basket. She planned to freeze some of them for chilled drink garnishes and to muddle some with satsumas for bourbon smashes like the ones she'd had a couple weeks ago with Ashley. No sense letting a good drink inspiration go to waste.

She sighed and answered, "I haven't called her yet."

Doug cast his eyes downward.

"Don't look at me with that tone of voice," she said. "I just haven't had time."

"Mm-hmm. Haven't had time or haven't made time? Having second thoughts?"

"No," she snapped. "And don't you dare ask me if I'm thinking she was right. This doesn't mean anything other than I'm forgetful. I'll call the adopter when I get home."

Doug put his hands on her shoulders and waited until she raised her eyes to look at him. "I know this is hard. This whole damn month is hard. And I know you're feeling betrayed and no matter what you say, the whole world could see that woman was more than a dog walker to you. But this *will* pass. And we'll all be here to help you through it." He pointed at the refrigerator case behind him. "Just not with blue cheese."

She laughed. "I get it, I get it."

"Listen, we can do a whole blue cheese-themed meal next time. We just aren't topping our Christmas Eve salmon with that funky shit." He faked a violent shudder running through his body. Then he turned serious and gave her a sideways look that Madison absolutely did not like the look of. "Maybe by the next dinner you'll have kissed and made up, and I can finally meet this magical dog trainer of yours."

"No." Madison started pushing the cart towards the checkout aisles. If she forgot something, she'd pick it up in the morning. But this trip and this conversation and her nonexistent relationship with Ashley were all finished.

Except she wasn't sure how she was supposed to be finished with something she couldn't stop thinking about.

She stood in a line and waited. She didn't know why she was letting herself get so upset. Heck, she didn't know why she'd let herself get in this mess at all in the first place. She'd already had her one good shot at at perfect relationship. She should have known better than to hope lightning would strike twice.

Doug followed and stood behind her in line. "Whatever you say. But from where I'm standing, it looks like you're the one who needs convincing that a reconciliation isn't in the cards, not me."

"There are no cards, and I don't need convincing of anything."

"All right, all right." They moved forward, and he reached in the basket to put the salmon on the checkout counter. "I just want you to be happy. Whatever that looks like for you, love."

She relaxed her shoulders and placed her bag of oranges on the belt. "I know you do, and I appreciate it. I appreciate everything you've done for me this past year. Really, I do. And this..." She gestured at the cart and the store around them. "This is making me happy again. Planning things and surrounding myself with you and our other friends and getting out of my apartment and out of my own head..." She took a second to catch her breath. "*This* makes me happy."

"Good." Doug bumped her arm gently with his own. "Because you're stuck with me."

She laughed. "Wouldn't have it any other way."

Which was completely true, even if she did secretly wish other things had gone a different way.

ASHLEY TURNED sideways to examine herself in the mirror behind her bedroom door. She smoothed the front of the slim royal blue blazer over her sparkly black tank and dark stretchy skinny jeans, tapping the toes of her black booties as she turned and checked herself out. Bi-chic, she liked to call her style. And it was about as festive as she was going to get *this* Christmas Eve.

She picked out a pair of sparkly clear crystal dangling earrings, then sat on her bed and began the job of inserting them. Not exactly the easiest task considering she only wore earrings maybe once a month, and her ear holes had a strict "use us or lose use" policy.

"Knock knock," Theresa said as she let herself into the room, rushing to sit on the bed squished against Ashley's side.

"Yes, please, do come in."

Theresa ignored the remark and held out her phone. "I found our soul mate."

"Please tell me this isn't another new hookup app."

"Sort of," she said with a lift in her voice. "But I promise you'll want to check this one out."

She tapped the screen and a photo of the most adorable gray kitten popped up. He looked like he was trying to high-five a reindeer statue.

"As soul mates go, he looks like a keeper."

"Don't get mad, but we're pre-approved. We just have to go down to the rescue center in person to meet them first. We can take him home the day after Christmas."

"We can't get a kitten. Not yet."

"Wait, not yet?" Theresa looked sideways at her. "Well, that's a new argument at least. What are we waiting for now?"

"We're waiting to figure out if I'm getting a dog."

"I thought we couldn't have a dog with our lease?"

"We can't."

"So…what? You want to move and get a dog? How does this—" Theresa's eyes widened with realization. "Hold up. A dog or *the* dog."

"*The* dog," Ashley repeated. "I have to make this right

somehow. If I screwed up the adoption and Madison really can't bear keeping him, I need to fix this."

"And what about making things right for you?"

"I messed up. I don't get right. I get to be the fixer."

Theresa frowned. "Who's going to make things right for you, if you don't?"

No one.

Theresa had a point, but Ashley couldn't fix things for herself this time. And certainly, no one would fix anything for her. Not after she'd made a mess of everything.

Not only had she lost Madison and Bacchus—both of whom she missed terribly—but she'd also lost her job. And since she hadn't been searching for a new one like she should have been doing the last couple weeks, the cash she'd been accumulating would quickly vanish before the end of the month.

She had options. If she wanted to, she could even try to get another dog walking job. Maybe hustle some dog training jobs in her own neighborhood, since she doubted she'd get a reference from Madison. She certainly wouldn't ask for one.

Then there was that other option she'd been considering...

Working on Madison's website had made her wonder if maybe she wanted to get back into that kind of work. But on her own terms this time. Maybe she could get over her fear of spreadsheets and actually run her own freelance thing making websites.

Maybe.

Nothing like that was on her five-year plan. Or any plan. But dog training hadn't been on any plans either.

Either way, she'd burned bridges and had to move on. As much as she wanted to, she couldn't change what she'd broken between her and Madison. She'd lost her chance and she had to accept that, no matter how much she'd miss having Madison in her life. She couldn't fix that. And she hadn't even accomplished the one thing she'd set out to do: keep Madison and Bacchus together. She'd failed at everything.

But maybe there was still one thing she could fix.

"Can you get a ride to the party later?" Ashley asked.

"Yeah, sure. What's wrong?" Theresa frowned. "You're already dressed and everything. Don't tell me you're gonna mope around here with these earrings on."

"I need to do something first."

"Something?" Theresa raised an eyebrow. "Or someone?"

She wished. "Something. Someone isn't an option anymore."

"Of course I can get another ride. But don't give up on the someone part. Not yet. Not for good at least." She put a hand on Ashley's shoulder. "Do the something. Then give her time. Maybe there's still a chance."

"I really doubt that."

"Hey, aren't you the one who believes in Christmas magic and all of that nonsense?"

At one point, Theresa would have been right. But not this time.

"I don't think even Christmas magic can fix what I've done. But I have to do the right thing anyway."

CHAPTER 13

MADISON STOOD IN HER LIVING ROOM FACING HER FRONT door and took a long, deep breath. She smoothed her black blouse again, inspecting it for stray bits of cracker crumbs and Bacchus hair, while her heart raced and her pulse pounded in her ears.

Why had she agreed to do this?

"For crying out loud, just open the door," Doug shouted behind her. "It's freezing out there."

Madison shot an icy stare over her shoulder.

Troy sat beside him, his skinny legs draped over Doug's knees. He playfully smacked the side of Doug's arm. "Leave her alone. It's not like she's going to leave them out there all night." He made a grimace. "Are you?"

Madison shook her head, unable to form words.

Troy raised his wine glass in the air. "Good. Go on, honey. We're here for you. Aren't we?"

"Always," Doug said, giving her an encouraging nod.

Of course they were. They'd been there for her more than she could ever repay. Not that they would ever expect repayment of any kind. But the free booze and food tonight was a start.

She took another deep breath and gripped the doorknob as the bell rang out through the apartment once more. She turned the handle and flung open the door with a giant smile on her face. "Hey! Come on in."

She'd hoped to see Lydia first, but she'd texted to say they were stuck in Mid-City traffic.

But she knew this trio of faces almost as well. Old friends from college. Former regulars to her and Callie's dinner parties. Only it was just Madison now. It would always be just Madison now.

"Hey, darling." Jerome, one of her oldest friends and a fellow photographer, bent and embraced her with his long, lanky arms. "I am *so* glad to be here."

"I'm really glad you're here." And she was. The moment she saw him and the others, everything made sense again. Doug and Troy had been right to push her. She needed this, to have these people here.

She exchanged hugs with the two women, Lila and Essie, entering behind Jerome and gestured inside toward the couch. "I believe you all know these two."

Jerome was already shaking hands with the pair. Essie said, "Been too long, I think I forgot."

"You wish," Doug teased.

They all hugged and laughed as Madison shut the door and watched from a distance. She'd had nothing to be afraid of. These people loved her and each other, and there was nothing for her to do but be in their presence, absorbing their energy.

"Oh, here. This is for you." Lila walked over and wrapped a gauzy green scarf hand-painted with strings of Christmas light bulbs around Madison's neck. "For our bright, shining hostess."

"It's beautiful, thank you." She held the ends up and examined Lila's artwork. It was so cute and festive. Ashley would have loved it.

Except she wasn't supposed to be thinking about Ashley this evening. Technically, she wasn't supposed to be thinking about Ashley at all, but especially not this evening. This evening was for old friends and new beginnings.

She surveyed her living room and thought about how different this place was from this time last year. How far she'd come.

She had decorations. Music. Party food. Friends.

Everything was perfect.

Or, at least, it should have been perfect. For some reason, she couldn't shake the sense that no matter what she filled this place with, something would always be missing. She'd been blaming that on Callie's absence, but this evening was reminding her that Callie's spirit would always be with her. That she and these people would always carry Callie's memory.

She looked down at the scarf again. The scarf that reminded her of another missing guest.

No, if that was what was missing, then she'd have to learn to live with that. Without *her*.

EVERYONE HAD SETTLED in with drinks and snacks, mingling in little pockets around the room. Troy and Doug had brought the most scrumptious looking salted caramel cheesecake that was chilling in the refrigerator.

She had to admit, it felt good having everyone in her

home again, surrounding her with laughter and love. She really should have done this months ago. It might have helped speed her healing along a little faster.

Then again, maybe her healing took exactly the time it needed.

Bacchus licked her fingers, and she bent to scratch his head. No matter how much she'd tried to deny it, Ashley had been right about one thing: Bacchus had been a key part of that process…just not the way Ashley had thought.

She stared at the print she'd picked up from the framer on her way home from shopping yesterday. It had arrived on her doorstep late last week, and she'd gone cold when she saw it as if she had been staring at a ghost. Two ghosts, really. It was a print from the same artist who'd done the one in her guest bedroom, the one she'd told Ashley that Callie loved so much. This one was another city painting…featuring a Calliope Street sign. She asked around, but no one claimed the gift, so she figured Ashley must have ordered it before their fight.

Her first instinct had been to send it back. She couldn't keep a gift like that. Not the way things had ended. But it really was perfect. So she decided to keep it, have it framed, and hang it up for the party. She'd planned to call Ashley to thank her and offer to pay her back for it. But she'd never mustered the courage to make that call.

There would be time. After Christmas.

Doug sidled up to her. "It looks great in here."

Madison nodded and took a sip of her orange-cranberry bourbon smash. She'd chosen to ignore her history with it, and allowed it to become her favorite drink this holiday season.

"Remind me again," he said, "why I'm looking at this print and not at the thoughtful woman who gave it to you?"

That was the question, wasn't it? Especially when Madison couldn't stop thinking about that woman *or* the kiss they'd shared.

"You know why."

"I know why you were angry at her. Justifiably so. But what I don't know is why you're planning to hold that mistake over her and cut her out of your life forever." He looked back and forth between Madison and the print. "Or maybe not forever after all?"

Madison frowned. "I don't know anymore."

In truth, she'd been asking herself those same questions ever since that gift showed up on her doorstep.

She was still upset with Ashley's actions—her overstepping and making a decision for Madison. But maybe she'd overreacted just a bit, because seeing this perfectly selected print reminded her of all the good Ashley had brought into her life. All of the support and friendship and laughter and cheer and pure joy. While she'd leaned on Doug for support and friendship this past year, she'd allowed very little of those other things in. But Ashley had barged right in and brightened the dark corners of Madison's life again.

She'd been so caught up in the idea that the universe was sending her a message by taking Callie away, that maybe she missed the message it was trying to give by sending Ashley to her.

"You know." Doug put a hand on her back and leaned in close. "You just need to leap."

Leap. Ten lords a-leaping. She could practically see Ashley standing on the chair across the room while they were hanging lights during the ice storm. She'd started singing "The Twelve Days of Christmas" at the top of her lungs until Madison joined in. Madison hadn't felt that light or happy in so long.

She'd be an idiot to ignore everything Ashley had brought into her life and only hold on to the one negative. The one mistake Ashley had made. Surely she deserved a second chance. Didn't they both deserve that?

"Maybe you just need some Christmas magic?" he added.

Madison chuckled. "You two would definitely get along."

"Looking forward to it," he said, giving her a wink.

The doorbell rang out over the music. It had to be Lydia and Camille. Madison turned to answer the door, but Troy was already reaching for it.

"I've got it."

Madison turned back to face Doug. "I'll call her next week. Before the new year."

He frowned and raised a judgmental brow.

"I will," she insisted. "I need to thank her for this anyway."

He seemed satisfied with that answer at least. He opened his mouth to say something else or to make some other demand, but shut it and looked curiously at Troy and the front door. Madison turned and saw Troy gesturing for someone to come inside. She couldn't see who was at the door, but if it had been Lydia, she would have already found her way inside, hunting down the promised cheesecake while hugging every guest along the way.

Madison walked to the front door, trying to hear the conversation over the music, but the only voice she could distinguish was Troy's insisting this new guest should come inside.

"It's freezing out there," he said. "Here, come inside while I get her."

He opened the door wider and stood aside, giving Madison a full view of Ashley on the porch. She was shivering, her pale cheeks and nose pink from the cold, and she held her thick parka-covered arms tightly around her body.

When her eyes found Madison, they both froze and stared at one another.

Madison shook free of her shock and stood beside Troy. "I've got this. Thanks."

He caught the tension and looked back and forth between the two of them, then he put a hand on her back and spoke softly. "You sure?"

Madison's heart pounded in her chest, louder than the driving beat of the boy band Christmas tune blasting through the living room, which she could barely hear over the blood rushing to her head now. She gathered her courage and nodded, her eyes still glued to Ashley.

"I'm sure."

CHAPTER 14

Ashley stared at Madison as she stood beside the skinny man with kind eyes. The man gave Madison's arm a squeeze before disappearing behind the partially opened door. Festive music played inside over the roar of joyful conversation and laughter. Beautiful. Exactly what Ashley had wanted for Madison.

Madison grabbed a coat from the hook on the wall and moved through the doorway onto the porch. "Sorry," she said, slipping her arm into a coat sleeve. "It's quieter out here."

"I'm just glad you didn't slam the door in my face." Ashley hugged her coat tightly to her body. She'd never felt so cold or so naked and exposed than she did at that moment. But she came here to make things right, so she kept her feet firmly planted and nodded toward the door. "I'm sorry for interrupting. I forgot about your party."

Madison's mouth wiggled like she was fighting a smile. "I believe you. I'm just shocked you would forget about a *Christmas* party."

"Yeah, well, I haven't exactly been myself lately." She quickly averted her eyes, embarrassed to reveal her pain.

Madison shifted her stance nervously. "I wanted to call you anyway. To thank you. For the gift."

Ashley felt her heart swell and fought to keep it in check. "It was a thank you. For giving me the job when I was grossly under-qualified and shockingly out of my depth. For believing in me."

"Anyone would have been out of their depth with that dog." Her warm smile was almost too much to bear.

Ashley pulled the key from her pocket and held it out. "I just came to return your spare key." She took a deep breath and continued. "And to say that I'm so sorry. It wasn't my place to talk to the adopter and I overstepped. There's no excuse. But I came here to tell you that I wasn't planning to force you to do something you didn't want to do or you weren't ready for. If you can't keep Bacchus—if you both need freedom and a fresh start—I'd love to adopt him myself."

Madison tilted her head, her eyes narrowing in confusion. "I thought you couldn't have a dog?"

"I've already spoken to my roommate," Ashley said. "We'll look for another place."

Madison's face softened, and a hint of shock settled in her eyes. She looked down at the key now in her hand. "I…I don't know what to say."

"You don't have to say anything right now," said Ashley. "I just need you to know that I'm sorry. I always wanted to do the right thing, whether that meant keeping you two together or taking care of him myself. And I messed up." She bit her lip. "When I saw you happy, I wanted to do whatever I could to continue making you happy. And I thought keeping Bacchus would do that."

Madison frowned. "You were wrong." She reached out for Ashley's hand and held it, her icy fingers somehow warming Ashley's hand and radiating heat all the way up her arm. "As much as Bacchus was growing on me, he wasn't the reason I was happy again." She lowered her forehead and stared into Ashley's eyes. "*You* were the one making me happy again."

Ashley's breath caught in her chest as she searched Madison's face for some sign that she'd misheard her. Surely her ears were playing tricks on her. Maybe her brain had attached some lyrics from the music inside to a piece of their conversation. Whatever it was, her conscious brain couldn't hear it.

But maybe her subconscious was picking it up. Because Madison couldn't have just said that.

"I'm sorry. I…I thought you said something else."

Madison shook her hand gently. "No, you didn't mishear me. I said you made me happy. You reminded me how to live again, how I needed to surround myself with people who made me feel happy and alive." She paused, then said, "And you showed me how to love again. I think that's why I panicked after that kiss. I felt like I had rushed things and hadn't quite come to terms with my feelings, but those feelings were still real."

Ashley stood frozen, absorbing every word.

Love.

In all the dreamt up Christmas miracles Ashley had ever played out in her head, none of them came close to this.

Madison laughed nervously. "Please, say *something*."

Before she could slow down her brain or her heart or the rest of her, Ashley blurted out, "Good."

Madison smiled. "Just…good?"

It was Ashley's turn to laugh, nerves and relief washing

over her in an anxious soup of emotions. "Good, because I'm head over heels in love with you, Madison."

Madison's hand squeezed around hers, and a smile spread across her face. Ashley moved closer and their icy lips met, kissing each other softly as warmth poured into every inch of Ashley's body right down to her frozen toes.

They held each other close, eventually ending the kiss and staring into one another's eyes again. This time, there was no hint of a mistake. No second-guessing.

Madison brushed a strand of hair away from Ashley's face, and Ashley's skin tingled against the touch of her fingers. Then Madison brought the hand she was still holding up to her lips and kissed Ashley's fingers. She nodded toward the door. "Come on, there are some people I'd love for you to meet," Madison said. "Plus, I'm sure Bacchus would kill me if I didn't bring you inside to see him."

Ashley laughed. Then she remembered the first part of their conversation. The reason she'd come here. "Wait. What about Bacchus. I meant what I said about wanting to take him if you can't. I can't bear to see him with anyone else."

Madison slid her hand against Ashley's face and gave her another soft, quick kiss. "Don't worry. Bacchus isn't going anywhere." Then she gave a sly grin. "And neither are you tonight."

She took a step backward and pulled Ashley toward the door. With her heart fluttering and her feet practically floating along the porch floor, Ashley followed Madison's lead inside, knowing she would follow this woman anywhere from now until the end of time.

EPILOGUE

Ashley entered the kitchen where Madison was assembling a plate of olives, pickles, and homemade pickled cauliflower with a shot glass filled with toothpicks in the center. She walked up behind Madison and slipped her arms around the incredibly soft cream-colored sweater Madison wore, resting her chin over her shoulder and inhaling her new fragrance—hibiscus and jasmine. Light and sweet, just like the woman she'd grown to know and love.

Madison turned her head to give Ashley a quick kiss. "Can you grab cheeses and start setting those out?"

Ashley gave another quick kiss in reply then released her. "Sure. Do you have a tray you want me to use?"

"Bottom left cabinet."

Ashley found the tray and gathered the cheeses from the fridge and the ones on the counter. As she arranged everything, she couldn't help but think how much this reminded her of that icy night they'd spent here, decorating and cooking pasta together. The beginning of everything.

And now they were spending New Year's Eve together.

Celebrating a new year and more new beginnings. She couldn't have written a happier ending for herself.

Bacchus wandered in and sat patiently at Ashley's side, looking up at her with his adorable begging eyes.

Well, maybe that icy night hadn't been the *very* beginning of everything. This guy had been the catalyst, but that night had changed everything. That night was when she'd allowed herself to begin asking *what if*.

And now here they were. Together. Prepping for a party on New Year's Eve. It was more than she'd let herself hope for on that icy evening.

"Speaking of cheese," she said. "Are Doug and Troy bringing that incredible salted caramel cheesecake again?"

"Nope. But close," Madison said. "Troy found some recipe for a cheesecake dip, sprinkled with graham cracker crumbs with strawberries for dipping."

"Oh my gosh, that sounds delicious."

"As long as Troy keeps Doug's hands off of it, I'm sure it will be delicious."

"Okay, I think I'm done here. Do you want these in here or on the little folding table in the living room?"

"Living room," Madison said. Ashley grabbed the tray and paused on her way out for another quick kiss. Except that quick kiss lingered and neither of them seemed to want to end it.

"All right, all right, all right, ladies. We've got a party to prep, a new year to kick in, and all that jazz. There will be plenty of time for making out later." Theresa breezed past them in search of the corkscrew on the far kitchen counter. She was a gorgeous sight in three-inch yellow sling-back heels, black faux leather pants, and a royal blue crop-top sweater.

Ashley smiled against Madison's mouth, and Madison pulled back, giving a sly grin. "My offer to set you up with one of my friends still stands."

Theresa spun around, her eyes dancing beneath her shimmery gold eyeshadow as she pointed the corkscrew at them. "I am perfectly capable of pulling my own New Year's Eve something-something out of this evening." She gestured at them both. "But if you can find me some of *this* magic, I will gladly take you up on that."

"Challenge accepted," said Madison.

Ashley exchanged a knowing glance with her at those words, remembering how she'd said that same phrase to Madison not so long ago. The fact that they already had inside jokes between them made her happier than anything.

Inside jokes and cheese plates had *not* been part of any of Ashley's plans. Neither had making out with Madison or starting her own website building business. But she found herself starting the new year embracing all of those things anyway. Making new plans and ditching the road map to follow the path her heart led her down.

The doorbell rang out through the building. Theresa said, "Good. So let's see if we can't find future spouse material in this party pool." With a wink and a strut, she sashayed out of the kitchen to answer the front door with Bacchus following closely behind her.

"I suppose we should get out there," Madison said.

"I suppose." Ashley snuck one more kiss in, then she took Madison's hand and carried the cheese tray in her other hand.

Hand in hand, they walked to the front door to greet their guests. To begin a fabulous new year and the start of their new life together.

To read a bonus epilogue,
go to:
https://leighlandryauthor.com/nol-signup/

ALSO BY LEIGH LANDRY

NOL SERIES (SAPPHIC CONTEMPORARY)

Collie Jolly
(holiday prequel novella)

Because You Can

Sing the Blues

Here You Go

SAPPHIC ROMANTIC MYSTERY

Out to Get Her

PARANORMAL SAPPHIC ROMANCE

All My Hexes

ABOUT LEIGH LANDRY

Leigh Landry is a contemporary romance author who loves stories with happy endings, supportive friendships, and adorable pets. Once a musician, freelance writer, and English teacher, Leigh now spends her days writing and volunteering at an animal rescue center in the Heart of Cajun Country.

To learn more about Leigh, sign up for her newsletter, and receive a free book, visit: http://leighlandryauthor.com